The Curse of the Dybbuk Box

The Curse of the Dybbuk Box

Doug Hensley

CONTENTS

S topped on page 146 the last chapters are missing.

Curse Of The Dybbuk Box
By
Doug Hensley
    Copyright 2024
    Author's Note
When light and darkness meet, Mark and Lisa discover
a dybbuk box at a yard sale. The warnings of an elderly woman do not stop them from unleashing a malevolent demon by opening it. The series of horrific happenings persuades them to seek the help of a Jewish rabbi who discloses the history of the box in dark lights and the only way to fight the demon inside.

As their lives are unraveled in a spiral of terror, Mark, Lisa, the rabbi, and a cast of captivating characters join forces to battle the forces of darkness. Together, they navigate a treacherous path, confronting their own inner demons while battling supernatural threats that seek to tip the balance of the realm.

Through fierce battles, heartbreaking sacrifices, and unexpected alliances, the group learns the true power of unity and resilience. They establish an academy-a haven of knowledge and training-to prepare the next generation of protectors. Their efforts lead to the formation of a council, uniting different species and realms, as they strive to bridge the gap between humans and supernaturals.

But when an ancient entity known as the Shadow Sovereign resurfaces, they face their greatest challenge yet. Their unity is tested, and they must confront their own fears and doubts to protect the realm from eternal darkness. In the midst of chaos, an unlikely ally, Valerius, emerges in search of redemption for his past misdeeds.

In one final, epic confrontation, they travel to a hidden temple to confront the Ebonheart: an ancient force with the power to plunge the realm into eternal darkness. Their bonds are tested, sacrifices made, and destinies intertwined as they unleash their combined powers to vanquish the darkness and restore balance.

"Shadows of Redemption" is a gripping tale of love, sacrifice, and the indomitable spirit of humanity. It explores themes of redemption, the power of unity, and the enduring hope that can be found in the darkest of times. Will Mark, Lisa, and their allies triumph over the shadows and pave the way for a brighter future, or will darkness consume them all?

Table Of Contents

Chapter 1: The Yard Sale

The hot sun beat down on Mark and Lisa as they strolled hand in hand down the suburban street. The idea of hitting yard sales on a lazy Saturday afternoon was just too enticing to resist. As they walked up to a dilapidated old house with weathered shutters and overgrown ivy, a sign caught their attention: "Estate Sale - Everything Must Go!"

Their curiosity was piqued, and Mark and Lisa exchanged excited glances between them as they hastened their pace. The yard was a chaotic display of forgotten treasures, with all the dust amassing on trinkets and forgotten memories. Among the sea of items, one peculiar antique wooden box stood out, its eerie aura drawing them in like moths to a flame.

As they reached the box, the old woman running the sale appeared beside them, her frail frame barely visible under layers of faded clothing. Her voice trembled as she spoke, "Be careful with that box. It's a dybbuk box. It may harbor a demon within."

Mark and Lisa exchanged amused glances-there was more humor than alarm in that warning. "A demon?" Mark chuckled. "Come on, it is but an old box-what harm could it cause?

The old woman's eyes filled with concern, her gaze pleading with them to take her words seriously. "You don't understand. This box has a dark history, a malevolence that has plagued my family for generations. Please, I beg you, leave it be."

Lisa, ever the skeptic, smiled and placated the old woman. "We appreciate your concern, but we don't believe in demons. We're just looking for something unique to put in our home. We'll take it off your hands for five dollars."

The old woman paled, but she seemed to accept the offer as if resigned to some awful fate. Her eyes clouded with concern. "Very well, but remember, you have been warned."

Amidst the buzz of excited shoppers and the clinking of coins, Mark and Lisa paid for the box and took their new treasure home. The weight of the box was strangely comforting in Mark's hands, as if it held a secret waiting to be unraveled.

As they entered their cozy living room, with eclectic furniture and cherished memories, Mark and Lisa carefully set the box on their coffee table. The room seemed to darken as they observed the intricate carvings on its weathered surface. Strange symbols, etched into the wood, hinted at a history far more ominous than they could fathom.

Curiosity got the best of them. With trembling hands, they reached for the lid; a mixture of anticipation and trepidation swirled within their hearts. The creak of the lid being pried open echoed through the room, with the stale air carrying the chill of foreboding. But with the releasing lock, unbeknownst to them, something lay dormant-no longer-which stretched ethereal tendrils into unsuspecting lives. The coldness in that room now felt as though some evil entity had tainted the air they breathed.

A deep feeling of foreboding seized their bones as Mark and Lisa peered into the blackness within. It seemed to hold a malevolent spirit, no longer containing an energy that seethed with malice. Still, they laughed it off, finding ancient tales of demons superstitious.

"See, nothing but an empty box," Mark scoffed, trying to get rid of the nagging doubts that gnawed at the corners of his mind. But as the lid swung open further, a gust of wind ripped through the room, blowing out candles and casting eerie shadows on the walls. An inexplicable sense of dread washed over them, but it was too late to turn back.

They had, unwittingly, set in motion an unending chain of events that would change their lives forever.

As the shadows deepened and the room grew thick with an otherworldly presence, the couple felt an unseen entity watching their every move. A whisper, barely audible, brushed against their ears like a ghostly caress. Goosebumps prickled on their skin, and a chilling realization began to dawn upon them-the old woman's warning held truth.

The atmosphere thickened, with the once-familiar room appearing alien and hostile. Crackling with anticipation, this silence was pregnant with something dark to come. This was something beyond their surmise-something ancient, almost as old as time, and mean.

But it was already too late to turn back a page. The demon that had been unleashed from a confinement of centuries was needy for chaos and despair.

Little did Mark and Lisa know, this would be the last semblance of peace that would remain for a very long time to come in terrors. The dybbuk box, once forgotten, became the very key to their darkest nightmares, and the demon inside would yearn for their souls.

Chapter 2: The Unseen Presence

The room fell into an eerie silence as Mark and Lisa stared wide-eyed at the open dybbuk box. A palpable sense of malevolence filled the air, making it difficult to breathe. Shadows danced on the walls, whispering secrets that sent shivers down their spines.

Mark's hand shook as he reached out and touched the box, his fingertips grazing the ancient wood. Suddenly, a surge of icy energy coursed through his veins, causing him to recoil in horror. Lisa gasped, her eyes wide in disbelief at the dark energy that seemed to emanate from the box and permeate their once-happy home.

"What have we done?" Lisa whispered, shaking with fear.

Mark swallowed hard, his mind racing to make sense of the inexplicable. "We.we need to put it back," he stammered, his gaze fixed on the malevolent presence that seemed to loom over them.

With shaky hands, they attempted to close the lid, but an unseen force pushed against their efforts. The box resisted their every move, as if the demon within reveled in its newfound freedom.

A cold gust of wind went through the room, blowing out what few candles were left to make them stand there in complete darkness. The only light was the dim, eerie glow of the moon through the curtains, with shadows dancing on the walls.

The couple huddled together, their hearts pounding in unison. The air grew heavy with an ominous presence, and a chorus of whispers filled their ears, taunting and mocking their feeble attempts to regain control. "Mark, we have to do something," Lisa whispered, her voice strained with desperation.

He nodded, his gaze scanning the room for any way of escape. But whichever direction he looked, the shadows seemed to be closing in on them. Their previously peaceful sanctuary had turned into a malevolent lair, and they were held captive within its clutches.

As the night wore on, the demonic presence became bolder, manifesting itself in an increasingly terrifying way: things levitating, doors slamming shut with such force that it rattled their very souls, a putrid stench penetrating the air. Whispers grew louder, morphing into sinister laughter that echoed down the empty corridors of their home.

Sleep became a thing of the past as Mark and Lisa entered the relentless battle with an invisible enemy. Fatigue gnawed at their bones, while their minds went into states of paranoia and hallucinations. They began to question their sanity as the line between reality and nightmare became one.

Days turned into a nightmarish blur of torment and fear. Their bodies weakened, their spirits tested to the brink of collapse. Desperation led them to the realization that they needed help, guidance from someone who understood the ancient forces they had unwittingly unleashed.

They remembered the words of the old woman that only one person could help them—a Jewish rabbi. Determined now, they began to reach out into their community in desperation for guidance and direction.

It was through some connections that they finally came across Rabbi Jacobson, a sage and highly regarded spiritual master renowned for his faith and knowledge concerning the occult. Mark and Lisa, even though disbelieving, still had one thread of hope-that this rabbi may hold the key to their salvation.

A meeting with Rabbi Jacobson was arranged in urgency. Down a narrow corridor and into a small study lined with ancient texts and artifacts of his faith, they came face to face with a man whose eyes reflected battles fought against the forces of darkness.

Mark and Lisa poured out their harrowing tale to an attentive rabbi whose features registered concern and compassion. His nods were affirmations to them of what they believed was the malevolent power of the dybbuk box and the demon within.

"You have unknowingly unleashed a force that thrives on fear and despair," Rabbi Jacobson said in a serious tone, his voice full of solemn authority. "But take heart, for the battle is not lost. We shall fight together to rid your lives of this ancient evil."

Mark and Lisa listened intently to the rabbi with renewed hope, seeking solace in every word he uttered, guided by his profundity. He reassured them that by faith, perseverance, and ancient rituals, their lives could be taken back from the demon.

Days merged with endless nights as Rabbi Jacobson looked for the sacred knowledge and incantations needed against the demon in every ancient text. Together, they prepared a plan-a perfect balance between spiritual war and faith.

The rabbi's presence had brought a new sense of security to the shattered lives of Mark and Lisa. His steadying guidance and refusal to abandon belief instilled hope within them, fuelling the determination to square off with the demon head-on.

In the bowels of their once-cherished home, a holy ritual was well underway. Candles danced, casting wraith like shadows on the walls as Mark and Lisa, led by the ancient wisdom of Rabbi Jacobson, prayed for protection and cleansing. The air was electric with tension as the demon felt its imminent danger. Its presence surged, testing their faith and resolve. The walls seemed to pulse with darkness, threatening to consume them whole.

But Mark and Lisa, buoyed by the rabbi's unyielding faith, held firm. They chanted ancient verses, calling for protection and banishment, their voices ringing with a strength they never knew they had.

With each word he spoke, the demon's grip weakened. Its screams of anger and defiance echoed through the halls, growing fainter with each passing moment. The battle for their souls raged on, but Mark and Lisa refused to yield to the darkness.

Finally, in a crescendo of holy incantations, the demon's malignant grasp started to weaken. Its presence shrank and pulled backward into the innermost recesses of the dybbuk box that had confined it for centuries.

As the last verse escaped their lips, the room was filled with an encompassing silence. Mark and Lisa fell onto their knees, their bodies weak yet their spirits victorious. They had confronted the demon head-on and emerged triumphant.

Rabbi Jacobson's face was lined with fatigue, but a deep satisfaction smiled in his eyes as he laid a hand on each of their shoulders. "You have conquered darkness, but don't be overconfident," he warned. "Evil never dies; it just waits for its next opportunity."

With the demon sealed once again in the dybbuk box, Mark and Lisa knew life would never be the same. They had seen humanity at its darkest, yet they had also seen what faith and the human spirit are capable of.

They said goodbye to Rabbi Jacobson with a renewed strength in themselves, like a beacon of hope that would see them through the uncertainty of the future. Their home, which had been filled with the shadows of despair, still lingered with the promise of healing and renewal.

Little did they know, the fight against the forces of evil had only just begun, and their lives would be inextricably linked with the ancient darkness they had let loose.

Chapter 3: The Lingering Shadows

Mark and Lisa stood in the aftermath of their battle with the demon, their bodies weary and their spirits scarred. The room felt heavy with the remnants of the malevolent presence that had plagued them for days. The dybbuk box sat once again shut on the coffee table, a constant reminder of the darkness they had faced.

Rabbi Jacobson watched them with a mixture of trepidation and admiration. He could feel their exhaustion, both physical and emotional, but he also saw the glimmer of strength that had carried them through the ordeal. He knew their journey was far from over.

"Mark, Lisa," the rabbi said softly, "you have confronted a true evil, and yet it is upon you to watch out. The forces of darkness are relentless, and they will seize upon any weakness that may allow them to rise once more."

Lisa nodded, her eyes reflecting both fear and resolution. "We know, Rabbi. We won't drop our guard. We're ready for whatever it takes to defend ourselves."

The rabbi smiled, appreciating their resolute spirit. "That is good to hear. But remember, you are not alone in this battle. Reach out for help when needed, and never underestimate the power of faith."

With those parting words, Rabbi Jacobson took his leave, promising to be available whenever they required his guidance. Mark and Lisa watched him go, grateful for his support and knowing that they had an ally in their ongoing struggle against the darkness.

As the days turned into weeks, a sense of unease settled over their once-happy home. Lingering shadows seemed to dance in the corners of their vision, and whispers echoed through empty rooms, as if the demon's presence still lingered, waiting for an opportunity to strike back.

Mark and Lisa tried to lead their lives as normally as possible, but the scars from this encounter ran deep. Sleep became a hazardous voyage into the unknown, with nightmares and restless visions. They knew the demon would not rest until it found a way to break free once again.

Determined to strengthen their defenses, Mark and Lisa burrowed into research. They read through ancient texts in search of knowledge about the dybbuk box and the rituals that could help them in this endless fight. With every word they read, it brought them closer to fathoming the depth of the darkness they were up against.

In that search for knowledge, they came upon other families who, throughout history, had also crossed paths with the dybbuk box. Each story told of chaos and devastation when the demon had been released.

Mark and Lisa realized their struggle was not unique but part of a larger tapestry of suffering caused by the malevolent spirit trapped within the box.

Equipped with this new knowledge, they returned home

\and armed it with protection-mezuzahs on every door, sacred amulets placed at every strategic corner of the house, and blessings uttered daily to ward off evil spirits.

But as days went by, it was evident that these precautionary measures were not enough; the demon's influence insinuated itself into the most trivial details of their lives.

The electronic equipment malfunctioned, casting an eerie, flickering light and distorting sounds in the house. Unexplained cold spots persisted, chilling their bones and reminding them of the relentless presence that haunted them.

Desperate for an explanation, they again approached Rabbi Jacobson, who heard their descriptions of the developing phenomena and the fear that had permeated their lives. The rabbi frowned, deep in thought over their problem.

"I fear that the demon has grown stronger," Rabbi Jacobson admitted gravely. "It has tasted freedom, and it will not rest until it finds a way to break free from its prison. We must take more drastic measures to contain it."

Mark and Lisa nodded, their decision made and their resolve firm: to do whatever it takes in order not to allow this demon to continue creating havoc in their lives and others.

Rabbi Jacobson contrived a plan-a hazardous, exhaustive

journey that would bring them to a hidden place of ancient power. There, in the bowels of a forsaken synagogue, buried deep in the woods, was a sacred artifact, a talisman, holding

within it the essence of light from above. It was their only hope in the ongoing battle against the demon.

The journey to the hidden synagogue was treacherous, filled with danger and uncertainty. They traveled under the cover of darkness, guided only by the moonlight and their unwavering faith. The woods whispered ancient secrets, and shadows seemed to reach out, testing their resolve at every step.

After what felt like an eternity, they finally reached their destination: the abandoned synagogue. Its façade was worn and weathered, like all things with a long story behind them. The air was crackling with ancient energy, and the smell of incense hung in the air.

They entered the hallowed halls of the synagogue, their footsteps echoing with reverence, as Rabbi Jacobson led the way. The walls were adorned with faded murals and crumbling texts, remnants of a once-vibrant spiritual community.

In the deepest chamber of the synagogue, bathed in flickering candlelight, the talisman awaited them—a radiant jewel encased in a sacred container. Its presence filled the room with an otherworldly glow, as if the essence of divinity itself resided within.

Rabbi Jacobson spoke the ancient prayers of protection, his voice booming with a power that seemed to emanate from the very core of his soul. Mark and Lisa listened as the rabbi invoked the ancient forces of light to infuse the talisman with divine energy.

With trembling hands, Mark and Lisa held the talisman, feeling its warmth seep into their very beings. It radiated a sense of power and protection, an armor to shield them from the demon's influence.

Armed with the sacred talisman, they returned to their home, their hearts filled with renewed determination. They knew that the battle against the demon would not be easy, but they were prepared to face it head-on.

Days ran into weeks, and weeks into months, but nothing seemed to stop the tireless attack of the demon against Mark and Lisa. The talisman stood to remind them that they did not struggle in their battle along. The demon's attacks grew with increasing fierceness, and their spirits were threatened with defeat. But they stood strong, firm in their faith and the sacred energy stemming from the talisman.

And as time went by, day after day, their bond grew stronger. They learned to anticipate each other's fears and weaknesses, supporting one another in moments of doubt and despair. Their love became a shield, protecting them from the darkness that sought to tear them apart.

Finally, the day of reckoning arrived. Mark and Lisa, armed with the talisman and guided by Rabbi Jacobson's unwavering faith, confronted the demon once again. This time, they were prepared to face its full wrath.

The battle was relentless and merciless.

The demon lashed out in fury, twisting their reality and distorting their perceptions. It whispered lies and stirred the deepest fears within their hearts. But Mark and Lisa, bolstered by their love and the divine energy of the talisman, fought back with unwavering determination.

With every incantation, with every holy gesture, the demon's power was fading away. It writhed in agony, its once-menacing form dwindling before their eyes. For a moment, it looked like a whirlwind created by the forces of light and darkness, shaking the very foundations of the room.

Mark and Lisa stood at the eye of the storm,

battered in body and spirit but their resolve unshaken.

Summoning the last ounce of their strength, they put all of it into one final, decisive strike. The talisman then shone brightly, rivaling the sun in its brilliance, and a brilliant light enveloped the demon with its divine embrace. A shrill scream echoed across as the demon was pushed backward, dissolving into nothingness.

The only sounds that filled the air were their irregular breaths and the light hum of the talisman. Mark and Lisa went to their knees, physically and emotionally spent, but a deep feeling of triumph swept over them.

Rabbi Jacobson approached them, his eyes filled with admiration and pride. "You have overcome unimaginable darkness," he said, his voice filled with reverence. "You have proven the strength of the human spirit and the power of unwavering faith."

Mark and Lisa exchanged a tired but grateful smile; their journey was not over, but they had again been rejuvenated. The demon had been defeated, but they knew they had to stay on guard because evil never dies-it only waits for an opportune time to attack.

In the days that followed, Mark and Lisa began t

o repair and rebuild. They welcomed love and

light into their home, wrapping themselves around the

positive energy of sacred protection symbols.

The experiences they had just had had strengthened them, and they purposed to live each new day with gratitude and resilience.

Rabbi Jacobson remained a steadfast presence in their lives, offering guidance and support whenever they needed it. Together, they conducted rituals to reinforce the seal on the dybbuk box, ensuring that the demon remained trapped within its ancient confines.

As time went by, the scars from their encounter with the demon began to heal, but they were forever marked by the profound lessons they had learned. They knew the fragile balance between darkness and light, and the need for vigilance against unseen forces.

Their struggle inspired so many other people who fought and are fighting their own battles, too, against the negative forces. Mark and Lisa, by their experiences and initiative, became beacons of hope, offering respite and guidance to persons who

came for their aid.

Their lives took on a new purpose as they dedicated themselves to helping others navigate the treacherous waters of the supernatural. They formed bonds with people who had their experiences with the dybbuk box or other malevolent entities, offering them strength and knowledge gained through their harrowing journey.

The dybbuk box was once a terror-inspiring object, but it became a relic of caution-a constant reminder of the power residing within the spiritual realms. Mark and Lisa kept it locked away, ensuring its confinement and safeguarding against any future release.

Years went by, and their story took a legendary turn: one that had been whispered to whoever searched for protection and guidance amidst darkness. Their names sounded synonymous with bravery and the ability to overcome; actions immortalized in annals of spiritual war.

Through it all, Mark and Lisa stood by their love for one another. They had been tried; the seams of their bonding had been torn apart, stretched taut by what they were forced to go through together. And they emerged, scathed, but the bonding fortified through the battles they went through together.

Their lives were now inextricably linked with the supernatural, yet they are hopeful for the future, with

a deep sense of purpose. As long as evil lurked in the shadows, they would be there, shining a light on the darkness and lending a hand to those who needed it most.

And so, their journey continued, marked by steadfast faith, unyielding love, and a commitment to protect others from malevolent forces that sought to sow chaos and despair. In a world where the line between reality and the supernatural grew increasingly blurred, they stood as beacons of hope, ready to face whatever challenges lay ahead.

And so, as their story whispered its way down through the ages, their names sewn in the fabric of history, Mark and Lisa were fated to play their role, their lives devoted to defending light against darkness.

Chapter 4: Unraveling Threads

Days turned into weeks, and weeks into months since Mark and Lisa had vanquished the demon and sealed the dybbuk box once more. Their lives fell into the semblance of normalcy; their home was tranquil and safe again. Still, a layer of unease remained.

Mark couldn't shake off the feeling that they were being watched, that out of the darkness, it still had its eyes upon them. Lisa, too, had her unsavory moments of paranoia, who was convinced the demon's presence had left an indelible mark on their lives.

One evening, as they sat in their living room, a loud crash startled them from their reverie. They leaped to their feet, their hearts pounding in their chests. Racing to the source of the noise, they found a shattered family portrait lying on the floor, its glass shattered into a thousand pieces.

And as if the evil entity's energy was seeking another

way in, their hearts became frightened once again. They needed to contact Rabbi Jacobson immediately for guidance and reassurance.

The rabbi listened intently as they described the incident, his brows furrowed with concern. "It seems that the demon's influence still lingers," he said, his voice weighted with understanding. "Sometimes, the bonds between our world and the supernatural are not easily severed."

Mark clenched his fists, frustration coursing through his veins. "But we thought we had rid ourselves of the demon," he said, his voice tinged with disappointment.

Rabbi Jacobson laid a reassuring hand on Mark's shoulder. "Banishing such a powerful entity is no easy task. It takes time, perseverance, and unwavering faith. We have to go deeper into the ancient rituals,

reinforcing the seals and protections."

Lisa nodded, her eyes determined. "We'll do whatever it takes," she said with resolution. "We can't allow the darkness to take hold again."

The rabbi nodded. His eyes shone with respect. "Together we shall take on this challenge once more, but be prepared-the way is dangerous, and the demon shall fight at any cost to freedom once more.

Days blended into nights, as Mark and Lisa, with the help of Rabbi Jacobson, scoured texts and consulted with other spiritual leaders who were experts in the occult. They searched out forgotten knowledge, hidden incantations, and talismans of protection. Each find brought them one step closer to the solution: a means of reinforcing their defenses against the demon's merciless assault. The rituals became more intricate and demanding, requiring unwavering focus and deep spiritual atonement. They said sacred prayers, cleansed themselves, and anointed their home with oils and holy water. The air crackled with energy as they forged a shield of light, determined to repel the darkness clawing at their doorstep.

But the demon was artful and tireless, always finding new ways to test their resolve. Shadows danced along the edges of their vision, whispers echoed through empty rooms, and nightmares plagued their sleep. The demon would seek to exploit their weaknesses, to sow doubt and discord among their ranks.

Consigned to this desperate fight against the engulfing darkness, Mark and Lisa could still find comfort in their steadfast love for each other and the unrelenting encouragement from Rabbi Jacobson. The challenges which life threw at them were unwavering, yet unbroken was their spirit, come what may.

It was on one fateful night, when they were performing

a protection ritual, that the demon struck an attack. The room had become cold, as if the very life force had been sucked out of the air. Objects levitated, swirling in a chaotic dance, as the demon's malevolent laughter reverberated through the room.

Mark and Lisa clung to each other, their minds filled with terror, but their resolve unshaken. Rabbi Jacobson's voice rose above the cacophony, his prayers piercing through the darkness. The sacred energy they summoned collided with the demon's malevolence, creating a tempestuous clash of opposing forces.

The battle raged further, the room a field of swirling energies and otherworldly beings. Mark and Lisa felt the weight of exhaustion upon their bodies, pressed to their limits. But deep at the core of their beings, an unyielding flame was burning-a fire nurtured by love, faith, and absolute belief in surmounting any obstacle.

Gaining from one final surge of strength in unison, they mounted their last attack against the demon. Their voices now joined together in one strong utterance-words ancient, yet ringing with a Holy Force that surged through their beings. The demon writhed and convulsed, contorting in agony.

The room was silent once again, as suddenly as it had begun. Mark and Lisa were panting, their bodies shaking in exertion. Weakened, conquered yet again, the demon took to the ether and vanished, leaving behind the mark of victory.

Tears of relief streamed down Lisa's face as Mark held her tightly, his heart filled with an overwhelming sense of gratitude. They had prevailed against the darkness once more, emerging stronger and more resolute than ever.

Before them stood Rabbi Jacobson, weariness etched on his face but shining bright with pride. "You have proven your strength and resilience," he said, his voice filled with admiration. "Together we have triumphed over the darkest of forces."

Mark and Lisa nodded, their hearts full of gratitude for the never-failing guidance and support of the rabbi. They knew that not all difficulties would disappear now, but they were ready to face them, standing strong with their faith unshaken and their love for each other.

As they set about repairing their shattered home, they knew that their journey was far from over. The demon may have been banished once again, but they knew the forces of darkness were relentless, always looking for an opening

to come back into their lives. But armed with the

knowledge and strength they had acquired through their battles, Mark and Lisa were ready for whatever lay ahead. They would remain vigilant in watching for the signs, seeking Rabbi Jacobson's guidance when needed.

Together, they would walk the thin line that separated their world from the supernatural, with a firm determination to protect their home and anyone who came for their help. The dybbuk box was a vessel of darkness and torment that would always remind them of battles fought and strengths found within themselves.

And so, as they rebuilt their lives and reclaimed their sense of security, Mark, Lisa, and Rabbi Jacobson stood as one-a beacon of hope in the face of unimaginable darkness. Their journey was far from over, but they faced the future with a renewed spirit of resilience and the unwavering belief that love and faith could conquer even the most malevolent of forces.

Chapter 5: The Veil of Shadows

Their hard-won victory against the demon did not blind Mark, Lisa, and Rabbi Jacobson to the fact that their battle was far from over. For one more time, the darkness had been pushed back, but they knew it would always seek a crack in their defenses, some moment of vulnerability to exploit.

They returned to their protections with a newfound determination to ready themselves and learn more about the supernatural. They pored over texts in search of hidden wisdom and forgotten rituals that could be used in their continuing battle.

The dybbuk box, once a source of terror, now became a focus of study and caution. Its mysterious origins and the demon it contained held the key to understanding the forces that had tormented their lives. They consulted with scholars and historians, piecing together fragments of history to unravel the box's dark past.

Their research led them to the story of Miriam, the old woman who had warned them about the box at the yard sale. They learned that she was the last surviving member of a lineage plagued by the demon's curse, the guardian of the dybbuk box for generations. Miriam had passed down the box, along with the warning, in the hope of preventing future calamities.

With a fresh sense of determination, Mark, Lisa, and Rabbi Jacobson sought out Miriam in the hope that she might be able to enlighten them further about the origin of the demon and any other forms of protection. They found her living in a small cottage on the outskirts of town, her eyes filled with both weariness and wisdom.

Upon coming through the door, Miriam greeted them with a well-mixed expression of both relief and trepidation because what burden lay upon her ancestral shoulders has now shifted to them; she felt the weight gradually getting shed. All sorts of her family's dark history-things that the demon inflicted, sacrificing to keep it contained-poured out.

"I have seen the darkness firsthand," Miriam said, her voice shaking with age and emotion. "It is a relentless force, ever hungry for chaos and despair. But you, my dear friends, have shown a strength and resilience that gives me hope."

Mark, Lisa, and Rabbi Jacobson listened intently as their eyes remained fixed on Miriam's weathered face. They felt a kinship with her, united by a shared burden and a determination to protect others from the demon's malevolence.

Miriam said the dybbuk box had been passed down through her family for centuries and that its true origins lost in the annals of time. Legends spoke of a cursed artifact, forged by dark sorcery and imprisoned with a demon's essence. It was said that the demon sought possession of the souls of all who dared to open this box, using them as vessels for its own wicked agenda.

With the dark history of the box laid before them, Mark, Lisa, and Rabbi Jacobson knew they would try every avenue to help in setting up their defenses. They pored over ancient texts in their search for forgotten rituals, the protective symbols that could give additional

strength to the barriers erected against the demon's influence.

This search led them to the "Guardian Sigil"-a powerful symbol that was able to create a spiritual barrier against the demon's attempts to breach their home. The sigil had

to be meticulously crafted, incorporating specific sacred geometry and infused with the energy of their intentions.

Guided by Miriam, they began a process of creation, which meant setting apart endless hours of effort into the minute design on a huge parchment. With every stroke came determination and love that transformed it into a talisman of protection.

Once the Guardian Sigil was complete, they set it in a place of prominence within their home, and its presence seemed to radiate a soothing energy that kept the darkness at bay. They now felt safe once more and hopeful, bolstered by the extra layer of protection they had forged.

But even with the sigil in place, they knew that the demon's cunning and persistence would not waver. They remained vigilant, alert to any signs of its encroachment. Shadows seemed to linger longer, whispers echoed through the night, and their dreams were haunted by fleeting visions of the demon's malevolent form.

Mark and Lisa decided to take an in-depth study of the nature of demons and the ways of engaging in the battle with them. They talked with experts in demonology, delved

into some ancient texts, and explored accounts of exorcisms and spiritual battles fought throughout history.

With this knowledge in hand, they were able to formulate a plan to fortify their spiritual defenses and prepare themselves for the possibility of another attack. They meditated and visualized, developing their ability to tap into the depths of their spiritual power. They also physically trained, building strength and endurance to match the demon's onslaught.

Months turned into years as Mark, Lisa, and Rabbi Jacobson worked ceaselessly to fine-tune their skills and delve deeper into the realms of the supernatural. They were a team that hardly found its match, the bond between them forged through shared adversities and their unflinching commitment to protecting the innocent.

It was during this time that they came into contact with people who had their own experiences with the dybbuk box and asked for their help. Mark and Lisa, empathetic and duty-bound, supported and helped t

hem through their struggles in fighting the forces of darkness. Their house became a haven, a place of refuge for those who were looking for solace and protection.

Feeling their strength increase, the demon began to struggle harder to break through their defenses.

The attacks became more frequent and heavier, testing their resolve and threatening to unravel their hard-won victories.

One terrifying encounter found the demon breaking

through their defenses and plunged them into a darkness that was impossible to penetrate. The air grew thick with malevolent feelings, heaving upon each breath. A cacophony of unearthly whispers bombarded their senses, and the demon's presence seemed to press in on them from every side.

But Mark, Lisa, and Rabbi Jacobson refused to give in. Drawing on their accumulated knowledge and unfaltering faith, they pushed against the suffocating darkness. Their voices rose unanimously in defiance, speaking ancient prayers of protection and banishment.

With a sudden surge of collective energy, they pushed the demon back and back until it was forced into the confines of the dybbuk box. The darkness dissipated, and serene calmness once again settled upon their home. They had emerged victorious, their spirits bruised but unbroken.

Still reeling from the encounter, Mark, Lisa, and Rabbi Jacobson realized that they had to explore alternative methods of permanently neutralizing the demon's power. They researched the ancient practice of soul-binding, seeking a way to sever the connection between the demon and the dybbuk box once and for all.

Their quest led them to an elusive spiritual guide, an elderly woman who was rumored to be able to bind wayward souls. With cautious hope, they approached her and shared their story with the wish that she would help them in their fight against the demon.

The spiritual guide listened intently, her eyes filled with a mixture of wisdom and compassion. She acknowledged the gravity of their quest and agreed to help them, but warned of the dangers involved. Soul-binding was a very delicate and dangerous practice, which required profound spiritual prowess and care.

Together, they had performed a complex ritual of conjuring ancient powers, channeling the energy of divine intervention. The spiritual guide wove her magic, her words and gestures aligning with the ancient rhythms of the universe. As the ritual reached its climax, a radiant light enveloped the dybbuk box, bathing it in a cleansing energy that severed the demon's connection to the physical realm. The darkness writhed and contorted, its power fading with each passing moment.

Mark, Lisa, and Rabbi Jacobson held their breath as they watched the demon's presence grow smaller and smaller. It fought the binding forces that held it fast, trying to break loose, but the spiritual guide was a master of his art in soul-binding.

In a final surge of energy, the demon uttered a shrill shriek, its essence dissipating into the ether. The room filled with a serene stillness, as if a heavy weight had been lifted off their shoulders. The battle had been won. The demon, now forever separated from the dybbuk box, would trouble them no more.

Mark and Lisa were overcome with emotion as the enormity of their victory sank in. Tears of relief streamed down their faces, their hearts filled with a deep sense of triumph and gratitude. Their journey, so marked by fear and perseverance, had culminated in the ultimate triumph of light over darkness.

Rabbi Jacobson stepped closer to the spiritual guide, his voice full of respect. "We are eternally in your debt," he said, his head bowed. "Your expertise and leadership have given us a new lease

on life from this evil entity.

The spiritual guide smiled, her eyes sparkling with pride. "It was your unwavering determination and faith that paved the way for this victory," she replied. "You have proven that even in the face of the darkest shadows, the light of hope can prevail."

The power of the demon had been neutralized,

and for the first time, the dybbuk box was bereft of its malevolent influence. Mark, Lisa, and Rabbi Jacobson were finally at peace and felt closure.

A chapter in their lives that was dominated by fear and uncertainty was over.

As they basked in the newfound tranquility, they knew their experiences had irrevocably changed them. They had seen the deepest darkness, faced their own fears, and emerged as warriors of light. Their hearts swelled with compassion and empathy, for they knew what it was like to suffer as so many others did in the same battles.

Their experience became the impetus for Mark, Lisa, and Rabbi Jacobson to commit themselves to the service of others in need. They established a network to help people who either had come into contact with the dybbuk box or other forms of malevolent entities. In coming together, they were able to provide a source of guidance, strength, and hope for those enshrouded by the forces of the supernatural.

Their home had been a battlefield of darkness but was transformed into a sanctuary, providing healing and protection. Welcoming any in need, they opened their doors to those in search of help or guidance amidst the unseen terrors that lurked in the darkness.

Years passed, and with time, the legend of Mark, Lisa, and Rabbi Jacobson only grew. Their names became synonymous with fighting the forces of the other side, known far and wide.

For expertise, unrelenting commitment to justice, and untiring care for the protection of others from dark forces, they were renowned.

Their journey had not been without sacrifice. Along the way, they had faced heartbreaking losses and endured their share of suffering. But the bond forged in the fire of their battles was unbreakable, and with each victory against the malevolent forces that threatened their world, their strength grew anew.

The dybbuk box, now nothing more than an artifact of caution, was sealed away in a secret chamber, its power contained and its secrets safeguarded. Mark, Lisa, and Rabbi Jacobson knew that their work would never truly be done, for evil would always exist in the shadows, waiting for an opportunity to strike. But armed with knowledge, experience, and unwavering faith, they stood as guardians of light, ready to face whatever lay ahead.

And thus, their story continued-both a testament to the resilience of the human spirit and the power of love and faith over any insidious adversary. From the darkest of depths they had emerged, forever changed but eternally determined to illuminate the path for others, lost in the veil of shadow.

As their story carried across the centuries, so did their names, in the chronicles of history, a beacon of hope: Mark, Lisa, and Rabbi Jacobson. The dybbuk box would be a lifelong reminder of their battles and victories-an homage to the indomitable human spirit and unyielding power of light.

Chapter 6: The Unseen Threat

The aftermath of their victory against the demon brought a newfound sense of peace and security to Mark, Lisa, and Rabbi Jacobson. Their lives had been forever changed by their encounters with the supernatural, but they no longer felt the immediate threat of the malevolent forces that had plagued them for so long.

But little did they know, an unseen threat lay in wait,

biding its time until the perfect moment to strike. The demon they had sent back was but a piece of a much larger puzzle, and the forces of darkness were far from defeated. First weeks grew into months, when one after another, mysterious events began to takeplace. These strange happening at their doors

hampered their regular life with doubt and fear.

Utterly unexplainably, something changed position, when alone, whispers would seem to echo in the air; night

dreams became nightmares with harrowing visions.

Mark and Lisa exchanged a concerned glance with Rabbi Jacobson; the thought was a heavy feeling in their hearts that this battle was far from over. And they reached out for their ally, Miriam, for guidance once again.

Weary and resigned, yet not defeated was the look of Miriam's aged face. "I have long dreaded that one day this day would come. The demon was just a pawn-a distraction from true malevolence baying to demolish our world."

Mark, Lisa, and Rabbi Jacobson listened intently as Miriam shared with them an ancient prophecy-one of a gathering storm, an impending convergence of dark forces that threatened to plunge the world into chaos. The prophecy, it said, was only a prelude to the demon they defeated-a more powerful one feeding on fear and suffering it would cause among humans. This was the Shadow King, a malevolent force that would tear asunder

he very fabric of reality, allowing darkness to spill into every corner of existence.

With these words, Miriam spoke out the weight that had just taken up residency in Mark's stomach. "What can we do?" he asked, his desperation not so very much far off. "How can we fight an enemy we can't even see?"

A spark of resolve danced in her eyes. "There is a way," she said, and for the first time, her voice was even. "But it will require a sacrifice-a joining of human and spiritual energy, a measured balance between the light and dark worlds."

Mark, Lisa, and Rabbi Jacobson looked at each other, the glint in their eyes mirroring their mix of resolve and trepidation. They knew the stakes were higher than ever before, and they were prepared to do whatever it took to protect their world from the encroaching darkness.

Miriam put them through a set of grueling preparations. They plunged deep into rigorous spiritual training, perfecting their skills and strengthening their ties with the supernatural. Their bodies and minds were stretched to the breaking point, the limits of their endurance tested as they delved deeper into the realms of the unknown.

And with each passing day, the veil between their world and the unseen grew thinner. They began to catch glimpses of the malevolence of the Shadow King, to feel his touch brush their souls like ice. Yet still they pressed on, against the dread that mounted within them.

And then, the day of the ritual finally arrived, when spiritswould converge and their human essence would merge with the forces of light. Mark, Lisa, and Rabbi Jacobson met at a sacred site, a place of ancient power known only to a select few. The air hummed with a palpable energy as they prepared themselves for the ultimate confrontation.

Under Miriam's guidance, they entered a trance-like state, their minds attuned to the ethereal currents that flowed through the universe. Their bodies shook with the strain of merging with the spiritual energies that surrounded them. They could feel the presence of the Shadow King-a looming darkness that threatened to consume their very beings.

As they chanted ancient incantations, their voices blended into a harmonic resonance that reverberated through the sacred space. The boundaries between reality and the supernatural blurred, allowing them to reach out and grasp the essence of the Shadow King.

Entwined were their spirits in a tenuous dance of light and darkness as they struggled to push their way against the encroaching malevolence. The surge of intensity in their struggle heaved their very soul with its weight.

Merged together, Mark and Lisa felt Rabbi Jacobson see what the true form of the Shadow King was: this towering figure wreathed in shadows, with eyes that burned with an unholy fire, an unstoppable presence threatening to overwhelm their minds and souls.

But in that, they found strength in the bond between them and a resolve unshaken. With every fiber of their being, they fought against the Shadow King's attempt to

overpower them, to extinguish the light that burned in their souls. As the struggle reached its crescendo, they unleashed a surge of pure spiritual energy, a blinding burst of light that seared through the darkness. The Shadow King let out a howl of fury and agony as its form disintegrated, vanishing into the void from which it had emerged.

Mark, Lisa, and Rabbi Jacobson collapsed to the ground, their bodies exhausted, their spirits spent. They had given all that they could give to this battle against the Shadow King and had prevailed.Miriam came to them, her eyes filled with a mix of relief and sadness. "You have done what few could ever hope to do," she whispered, her voice full of reverence. "You have defeated the Shadow King and prevented the cataclysm it would have brought upon our world.

Though physically weakened, Mark, Lisa, and Rabbi Jacobson felt a renewed sense of purpose. Their journey had been marred by so much pain and sacrifice, but they were stronger now than they had ever been.

In the aftermath of their victory, they knew that their work was far from over. The forces of darkness would always strive to tip the delicate balance between light and shadow. But they had proven themselves as beacons of hope, warriors willing to stand against the encroaching darkness.

Together, they would continue their vigilance, their dedication to protecting their world from unseen threats that lurked in the shadows. The sacrifices they had made, the hardships they had endured, all served as a testament to their unwavering commitment to the preservation of light. And so, as they recovered from their ordeal and prepared for the challenges that lay ahead, Mark, Lisa, and Rabbi Jacobson embraced their roles as guardians of the light. Their journey had taken them to the depths of despair and the heights of triumph, and they knew that their resolve would never falter.

Armed with the lessons learned from their encounters with demons, the dybbuk box, and the Shadow King, they forged ahead, ready to face whatever threat

dared challenge the sanctity of their world. The path ahead was uncertain, but they walked it heads high, their hearts filled with the unwavering conviction that love, faith, and the indomitable human spirit would always prevail over the forces of darkness.

Chapter 7: The Tangled Web

After their victory over the Shadow King, Mark, Lisa, and Rabbi Jacobson seemed to be caught in a web of intrigue and uncertainty. Their lives were so entwined with the supernatural that the sense of unease could not seem to leave them alone.Somber, they all gathered at Mark and Lisa's house, where the weight of the atmosphere was palpable. They had learned that the fight against darkness was not to be carried out in isolation; rather, there were those, both human and supernatural, who would seek to take advantage of the precarious balance between light and shadow.

There, their trusted guide and ally, Miriam, unveiled a set of decrypted documents she had found while doing her research. The documents hinted at a certain Order of Shadows, an organization that had existed for centuries, manipulating events from behind the scenes and drawing upon dark forces for its own purposes.

Mark fumed at the revelation as he internalized the gravity of Miriam's statement. "How can there be an organization that exists for the purpose of creating chaos and surviving on people's misfortunes?" he shouted exasperatedly.

Rabbi Jacobson nodded solemnly. "The Order of Shadows has existed for centuries, hiding from the world's eyes," he said. "Their thirst for power is endless, and they would do anything to maintain influence over the supernatural realm."

Lisa's eyes narrowed; her jaw set in an unyielding resolve. "We have to uncover the truth and dismantle this organization," she said. "They can't be allowed to continue their malevolent machinations."

With a new sense of determination, Mark, Lisa, Rabbi Jacobson, and Miriam plunged into the encrypted documents, deciphering the coded messages and unraveling the tangled web of the Order of Shadows. They found that the organization had infiltrated various aspects of society, manipulating events and pulling strings from behind the scenes.

Their investigations led them to a series of shadowy figures: high-ranking members of the Order who enjoyed positions of influence in government, finance, and the supernatural underworld. They knew it would be dangerous to expose the existence of the Order, but a sense of justice and protection for the innocent drove them onward.

The deeper they dug, the more their lives entwined with a network of informants and allies-people who had been hurt by the Order's evil and were anxious to see justice served. They became a clandestine resistance, a force determined to bring the Order of Shadows to its knees.

Their investigations uncovered a spate of ritualistic gatherings conducted by the Order-a congregation of dark energies aimed at manipulating the balance between light and shadow. Mark, Lisa, Rabbi Jacobson, and their allies knew that disrupting these rituals would be a crucial step in dismantling the Order's power.

With Miriam's guidance, they developed a plan to infiltrate one of these gatherings—an occult ceremony designed to tap into forbidden energies and unleash chaos upon the world. Disguised as loyal members of the Order, they would uncover their secrets, gather evidence, and expose the true nature of their nefarious activities.

The night of the ceremony finally arrived, steeped in darkness and secrecy. Mark and Lisa, along with Rabbi Jacobson and their allies, made their way to the hideaway, their hearts racing in anticipation and nerves. They moved through the labyrinthine corridors, footstepsquiet, purposeful.

As they entered the chamber where the initiation would take place, they were greeted with a scene of eldritch grandeur: candles flickering, sending shadows dancing around the room; symbols and sigils etched upon the walls pulsed with malevolent energy.

In the center of the chamber, a figure was shrouded in darkness: the Grand Master of the Order. His presence radiated the aura of power and malice, his eyes gleaming with a malevolent light. He sneered at the intrusion of their presence.

"You have stepped into a realm beyond your comprehension," the Grand Master hissed. He

spoke with the venom and arrogance of a serpent: "But you shall witness the true power of the Order of Shadows."

Yet defiant, Mark, Lisa, Rabbi Jacobson, and their allies stood undeterred. They had taken matters too far to let any movement of the Order send cold sweatsdown their backs.

Together they burst into the place in an influx of collective strength, their voices unified in ancient, praying sounds of protection and banishment broken as the light of intrusion

permeated it.With the power of his cohorts to feed him, the Grand Master let loose with a wave of dark energy. Shadows coiled and twisted, as if about to burst at any moment and overwhelm Mark, Lisa, Rabbi Jacobson, and the rest.

Yet they held firm- drawing from the source in the light and from each other in unity one final, defiant

blaze, they returned the Grand Master's attack-their combined spiritual energy against the darkness. The chamber became a battleground of light and shadow, each side vying for dominance.

With one last surge of determination, Mark, Lisa, Rabbi Jacobson, and their allies unleashed a torrent of divine energy that consumed the Grand Master. He screamed in agony as his form dissolved into nothingness, his power extinguished.

The room was silent, except for the ragged breathing of those who had overcome the darkness. They looked around, their eyes filled with a mixture of relief and vindication. A great blow had been dealt to the Order of Shadows, its leader vanquished, and their secrets exposed. But they knew that their battle was not yet won. The Order of Shadows was a vast organization with tendrils reaching far and wide. They would continue their fight, dismantling the remnants of the Order and seeking justice for those who had fallen victim to its malevolence.

As they regrouped and gathered the evidence they had collected, Mark, Lisa, Rabbi Jacobson, and their allies prepared to unveil the truth to the world. They would expose the Order's influence and ensure that those responsible for perpetuating darkness and suffering would face justice.

They had gone to the farthest depths of darkness in their journey of the supernatural and came back, not battered or bruised, but even more sure, even more resolute. United in their fronts, a beaming torchlight among invading shadows, ready to defy any obstacle that may stand on their path.

And so, with proof, will, and an unshakable belief in justice, Mark, Lisa, Rabbi Jacobson, and their associates pressed on to the next step of their mission-to expose the Order of Shadows and protect the world from its insidious grip. The road ahead was filled with danger, yet they were ready for whatever horrors lay in store at the bottom, for long ago they had learned one sure thing: that solidarity, love, and blind belief would always overcome evil.

Chapter 8: Shadows Revealed

The revelation of the Order of Shadows sent shock waves through the supernatural community and beyond. The evidence that Mark, Lisa, Rabbi Jacobson, and their allies collected was undeniable, showing the organization to be an evil influence, manipulating all levels of power for their own vile purposes.

News of the Order's exposure meant that a wave of fear and outrage surged through the ranks of the supernatural underworld; whereas earlier, those had silently suffered at the hands of tyranny, now the hopeful news of liberation consoled them.

Mark, Lisa, and Rabbi Jacobson knew they could not sit on their laurels. Dismantling the Order would take very strategic planning, alliances, and relentless pursuit of justice. They contacted other people and organizations

that had long suffered under the tyranny of the Order, uniting against the darkness.

The two formed an alliance that would attract the attention of several powerful supernatural beings who had silently watched the rise of the Order of Shadows. One such being was Morana, a formidable sorceress with ancient knowledge and a deep-rooted vendetta against the Order, who emerged from the shadows to join their cause.

Morana's presence brought with it a new sense of purpose and power to their ranks. With her expertise in ancient spells and her mastery over dark magic, she would turn out to be invaluable in their mission to tear the Order down and bring a semblance of balance to the supernatural world.

The two developed a comprehensive strategy

together: targeting key members of the Order and dismantling their operations piece by piece. They uncovered hidden caches of dark artifacts, disrupted rituals that fueled the Order's power, and brought to light corrupt individuals who had long operated with impunity.

This would become a battle with the Order of Shadows; one of cat and mouse where the leaders of such an organization were hunted down piece by piece. Each small victory would turn out to be a beacon of hope to stir others to rise and face up against the encroaching darkness.

In the course of their campaign, Mark, Lisa, Rabbi Jacobson, and their associates made a shocking

discovery-the true purpose of the Order. The Order planned to exploit a powerful artifact called the Shadow Heart, an artifact said to contain the essence of the Shadow King and grant its possessor unparalleled dominion over the forces of darkness.

Realizing the catastrophic consequences of the Shadow Heart falling into the wrong hands, they redoubled their efforts to find and secure the relic before the Order could wield its unimaginable power.

Their journey took them to ancient tombs, treacherous labyrinths, and forgotten realms where they encountered deadly traps and supernatural guardians. Mark, Lisa, Rabbi Jacobson, and their allies faced their own inner demons, confronting fears and doubts that threatened to undermine their mission.

As they journeyed deeper into the heart of darkness, their alliance was tested. Conflicts arose, fueled by differing ideologies and the weight of personal sacrifices. Yet, they recognized the importance of their shared goal and the strength that came from unity. Bonds were reforged, and they stood together, stronger than ever before.

At last, their tireless endeavor took them to the very bed of the Shadow Heart, laid within a chamber of quite ethereal beauty. Within it, the presence had become palpable and beset with danger. Therein, the relic did pulse with malevolent energies, a beacon of power ready to corrupt anyone who threatened to touch it.

They stood in a circle of protection, calling on the forces of light to shield them from the dark influence of the Shadow Heart. Mark, Lisa, Rabbi Jacobson, and Morana conducted a ritual that would seal the relic, neutralizing its power and ensuring it could never be used for nefarious purposes again.

The moment of climax during the ritual brought about

the shaking of the chamber and shadows that writhed

\across the walls. The air crackled with a mix of both anticipation and trepidation. Focusing their amassed spiritual energy, the synchronization of their hearts in purpose unleashed an outpour of power upon the Shadow Heart.

In a flash of blinding light, the artifact exploded into a thousand fragments, its malevolent energy dissolving into the ether. The chamber was silent now, the darkness receding as light triumphed over shadow.

Panting but victorious, Mark, Lisa, Rabbi Jacobson, and Morana caught their breath. The world was safe from the horrible power of the Shadow Heart. They had done it. But their task was not over. The Order of Shadows was still there, its people scattered but not beaten.

Unbeknownst to them, the remnants of the Order had regrouped, their leaders plotting a final, desperate bid for power. They sought to awaken an ancient entity, a malevolent force of unparalleled darkness, to unleash chaos upon the world and reclaim their dominance.

Mark, Lisa, Rabbi Jacobson, and Morana felt the threat of evil coming, a gnawing sense of unease settling upon their hearts. They knew that their final battle against the Order would be their greatest challenge yet, a culmination of their journey through darkness and their unwavering commitment to light.

With their new allies at their side and with the knowledge they had, they devised a plan for the final confrontation that would seal the fate of the supernatural world and the world in general. The will and spirit of their mutual determination were ablaze, shining bright to give hope to all those who had suffered at the mercy of the Order's tyranny.

Knowing well that their last mission would call for sacrifices, put lives into jeopardy, and the fate of all that they held dear in the balance, they nonetheless knew that with love, faith, and an unbreakable will, they would confront the Order of Shadows head-on, ready to face their darkest fears and overcome the shadows that threatened to consume them all.

Their journey had led them through heartache and triumph, testing their limits and shaping them into warriors of light. Now, with the fate of the world resting on their shoulders, they prepared to confront the ultimate darkness, to vanquish the Order of Shadows, and to ensure that light would forever prevail over the encroaching shadows.

Chapter 9: Confrontation at the Abyss

This was to be the final confrontation between Mark, Lisa, Rabbi Jacobson, their allies, and the remnants of the Order of Shadows. The air was thick with tension as they prepared for battle, one that would determine the fate of both the supernatural realm and the world itself.

The place of combat chosen was an ancient, desolate place-a bottomless chasm that existed at the edge of the known world. Its dark and dangerous depths were symbolic of the very heart of the Order's evil-an embodiment of the darkness they fought.

Huddled on the brink of the abyss, Mark, Lisa, Rabbi Jacobson, and their supporters shared a moment of solemnity. Eyes met, speaking volumes of unuttered resolve and unity. Each member of their group had a touch of the darkness in his or her own way, and now they stood united to face the final battle.

Down into the abyss, the haunting silence wrapped itself around them. The air thickened to an oppressive darkness, and wisps of malevolent energy whispered through the void. Shadows danced along the walls of the cavern in foreboding, erratic movements.

The remnants of the Order, under the guidance of their last surviving leader, Malachi, awaited them at the heart of the abyss. A fanatical gleam in his eyes, his voice echoed through the depths. "You have dared to challenge us, but you shall soon witness the true extent of our power," he declared, a chilling conviction carried in every word.

Mark, Lisa, Rabbi Jacobson, and all their allies stood in a line of defense, their united power shining like a shield to hold off the incoming darkness. Their souls were ablaze with unrelenting resolve, every step forward an attestation of their unshaken resolve to save the world from the clutches of the Order.

The battle erupted in a fury of arcane spells, supernatural powers, and the clash of weapons. Mark's fists shone with an otherworldly light as he unleashed devastating punches that sent shock waves through the opposition. Lisa connected with the elements, bringing gusts of wind and torrents of water down on her enemies. Rabbi Jacobson uttered ancient prayers, conjuring sacred symbols to dispel the darkness and protect his allies from harm.

Their allies fought with equal tenacity, each contributing their unique abilities and unwavering resolve. Morana unleashed torrents of dark magic, her spells weaving through the air like serpents, striking down their adversaries. Others among their ranks, skilled in combat or gifted with supernatural powers, fought with unwavering determination, their resolve undeterred by the malevolence that surrounded them.

The battle raged on, each side unveiling their full armory of abilities and strategies. Light and darkness collided with fierce intensity, the cavern echoing with the clash of metal and the chorus of incantations. The combatants danced with death, their every move a show of their strength and willpower. But as the battle wore on, the odds began to tip in the favor of Mark, Lisa, Rabbi Jacobson, and their allies. Their determination and unity proved to be an unassailable force against the fractured remnants of the Order. Slowly but surely, they pushed back the darkness, forcing their adversaries into retreat.

As the last remnants of the Order were penned in, their leader, Malachi, stepped forward, his face twisted into a deranged smile. "You may have won this battle, but darkness can never truly be extinguished," he spat, his voice dripping with venom.

Mark, Lisa, and Rabbi Jacobson came forward, their faces reflecting a mixture of fatigue and determination. "We stand as guardians of the light," Mark said, his voice firm. "And we will protect this world from the darkness you seek to unleash."

The eyes of Malachi blazed with wrath, and he released a surge of dark energy. But Mark, Lisa, and Rabbi Jacobson, drawing on the collective strength of their allies, stood firm against him. They formed a shield of pure light that repelled the darkness, sending its energy back at Malachi.

Back he reeled, the leader of the Order, as it is, his dark aura burning away with every hit; it became a scream of rage, in deepest frustration, as his strength fled-the light engulfed him, and in one last wild-grown exertion, he was gone.The abyss quivered as if the darkness was welling backward, recoiling from the defeated leader. The war was won, and there were no more remnants from the Order to be seen anywhere.

Mark, Lisa, Rabbi Jacobson, and those who supported them stood amongst the wreckage, battered bodies and wearied, but victorious spirits aglow. The abyss, a symbol of darkness, radiated a restored sense of hope and light.

After the battle, they took a moment to remember those who had died in the fight against the Order. They honored the sacrifices made, the lives lost in the name of justice and protection of the innocent.As they came out of the abyss, their way lit by the oncoming dawn, they knew that their work was yet to be done. Although the Order of Shadows was defeated, the world remained such that darkness could spread and grow in it.

Mark, Lisa, Rabbi Jacobson, and their allies pledged to remain vigilant, to protect the delicate balance between light and shadow. They would continue to stand as guardians, ever ready to confront the forces of darkness and ensure that hope would always prevail.

Their journey had been a tale of unwavering struggle, sacrifice, and triumph. They had faced the darkness

full on, stood and fought against their deepest fears, and emerged into a world threatened by shadows, shining as beacons. And thus, with the fire of purpose in their hearts, the strength of their unity leading, Mark, Lisa, Rabbi

So it was, as the next part of their quest-to restore and rebuild-began, with Jacobson and all others allied. They realized that this fight afterwards from the Order of Shadows was as huge as the fight itself.

News of their victory spread throughout the supernatural community and beyond. Those who had lived in fear and oppression under the Order's rule found renewed hope and began to emerge from the shadows. Without the

influence of the Order, new alliances were forged, and a network of support began to grow.

Mark, Lisa, and Rabbi Jacobson took on the mantle to guide and protect those in flight from what was left of the Order. They granted it sanctuary, a place where shelter and protection were afforded them from victimization and persecution.

They knew that the wounds left by the reign of Order would take time to heal. Many had suffered traumas

unimaginable and carried scars both physical and emotional. Mark, Lisa, and Rabbi Jacobson, drawing on their own experiences and strength of unity, offered comfort and sympathy to help others find their way toward recovery.

They used the momentum of their victory to engage with the wider supernatural community, working unceasingly to reinstate the balance and order that once was. They established councils and alliances that brought together various supernatural beings from realms and backgrounds to understand and cooperate with one another in peaceful co-existence.

Mark and Lisa, with their knowledge about the dybbuk box and the supernatural realm, took up the responsibility of keeping any dangerous artifacts and making sure they would never get back into the wrong hands. They set up a facility, locked tight, where these things could be stored and studied, creating a repository of knowledge that would help prevent such catastrophes in the future.

Rabbi Jacobson gained respect among the supernatural community for guidance, counsel, and spiritual support. His reputation as a wise and compassionate leader grew, and he was sought after to resolve conflicts and dispel the darkness that still lingered in the hearts of some.

Morana also played an important role in the healing and restoration process. She channeled her vast knowledge of magic and ancient rituals to restore balance to the supernatural realm, mending the wounds inflicted by the Order's reign. Her dedication to atone for her own past actions fueled her determination to help rebuild a world

free from darkness and oppression.

And they did together set out to rewrite the story of the Beyond. They would break the chain of fear and violence and, in its place, install comprehension, harmony, and mutual respect. Misconceptions would be dispelled and unity fostered among beings of the different realms

through education and outreach programs.

But their job was not without its challenges, as some remnants of the Order still lurked in the shadows, plotting and scheming to regain their lost power. The battle against darkness was not won in a day and they were ever watchful, prepared to meet whatever dangers arose.

As time went on, the supernatural realm began to change. The wounds inflicted by the Order of Shadows began to heal, and a sense of repair and rejuvenation took its place. The supernatural community found strength in unity and in the shared belief that darkness could be overcome by the collective power of light.

Mark, Lisa, Rabbi Jacobson, and their allies became legends, their names whispered with reverence and gratitude. They had faced the very depths of darkness, overcome unimaginable challenges, and emerged as beacons of hope and resilience.

It was not that their journey had been free of sacrifices;

friends and allies had fallen on their journey. But their memory lived on, inspiring future generations to stand against the encroaching shadows and fight for a world where love, compassion, and understanding reigned.

Over the next years, Mark, Lisa, Rabbi Jacobson, and their friends continued to work tirelessly in protecting the world against the forces of darkness. They faced new challenges and fought against emerging threats, always united by their unwavering commitment to safeguarding the delicate balance between light and shadow.

The legend grew, to be told for generations to come: the indomitable human spirit, and how the bonding of men stood strong against all odds. Mark, Lisa, Rabbi Jacobson, and their allies had thus proven that even in the darkest of times, hope may win and light shine

where there was only darkness.

And as they looked upon a world now changed, Mark, Lisa, Rabbi Jacobson, and the rest of their unlikely band of associates knew well that it wasn't just a journey of theirs alone, but part of the testimony of resilience within the human spirit-to remind all that love, faith, and unwavering resolve could conquer the most insidious of foes.

It was a story of triumph and redemption that would stay in the annals of supernatural history forever. As they pressed onward, against what life had in store, the bonds forged in the crucible of darkness stood sure guides to strengthen their resolve and point the way in those days of struggle to turn the tide against the shadows slowly crawling over the world.

Chapter 10: The Legacy of Light

Years had passed since the battle against the Order of Shadows, and the world had changed. Mark, Lisa, Rabbi Jacobson, and their allies had achieved what many thought impossible—they had brought light and hope to a supernatural realm once consumed by darkness.

The supernatural community had changed forever.

Alliances forged in the fire of battle had been tempered

into a united front against the forces of darkness. The memory of tyranny at the hands of the Order was a

reminder to be vigilant and protect the fragile balance between light and shadow.

Mark, Lisa, and Rabbi Jacobson had grown older, becoming the respected elders of the supernatural community, teaching and mentoring the next generation. Sharing in their knowledge, they had passed on the lessons of compassion, understanding, and unity that had driven their own journey.

But even in times of relative peace, the supernatural

realm held shadows in its corners. New threats emerged to challenge the hard-won equilibrium. The forces of darkness, which had sought to exploit the vulnerabilities of a healing world, rose to fill the void left by the Order's demise.

Mark, Lisa, Rabbi Jacobson, and their cohorts stood watch, never yielding. Again and again, they stood as beacons of light, preparing to fight against the newest challenges that would weigh heavily on the balance toward darkness. Their experience and expertise in combating new malevolent entities and working with tireless efforts to avoid another rise of tyranny became very important.

As they faced these new threats, a new generation of supernatural beings stepped forward, inspired by the legends of Mark, Lisa, and Rabbi Jacobson. These young warriors, guided by the teachings of their mentors, embraced the responsibility of protecting the world from supernatural malevolence.

Among them was Elena, a young witch with great powers and firm principles of justice. She had been drawn to the stories of Mark, Lisa, and Rabbi Jacobson and sought

them out for guidance, becoming their protégée.

Under their tutelage, Elena honed her magical abilities, combining the innate talent with the wisdom passed down from her mentors. She became a beacon of hope for those who had lost their way, standing as a symbol of resilience and determination in the face of darkness.

Elena's journey was not without challenges: formidable adversaries, ancient curses, and the consequences of an unchecked power. Yet at every turn, she was guided through and supported by Mark, Lisa, and Rabbi Jacobson, each hurdle overcome making her stronger.

In her search, Elena came across a secret sect amongst the supernatural-a fanatic cult named the Sons of Shadows. This group had risen from the ashes of the Order, seeking to resurrect its dark agenda and plunge the world into chaos once again.

Elena's revelation sent shock waves into the supernatural realm. The echoes of the past had resurfaced, and it would seem that the peace and harmony they had struggled so hard to achieve could unravel at any moment. It was a stark reminder that the battle against darkness was never truly over.

Mark, Lisa, Rabbi Jacobson, and their allies joined

Elena against this new threat. Together, they marshaled

their knowledge and resources in an effort to defeat the Sons of Shadows and destroy their dangerous ideology.

Their confrontation with the Sons of Shadows led them to ancient catacombs buried beneath layers of forgotten history. The air was heavy with the lingering presence of malevolence, as if the very walls whispered of past atrocities.

There, in the very center of the catacombs, a large chamber was waiting. Its walls were decorated

with signs of darkness, and a sinister altar stood in the middle—a medium between them and the malevolent energy that fed the Sons of Shadows.

Emerging from the shadows as they entered the chamber, the Sons of Shadows had fanatical zeal burning in their eyes. Commanded by a charismatic but insane leader named Malakai, they vowed to restore the Order's

glory and bring chaos upon the world.

What then transpired was a fierce, relentless battle. Mark and Lisa, Rabbi Jacobson, along with their allies, used skillful strategies and unshaken resolve in their attack. Elena's new powers, sharpened by their help, proved to be key to winning against the Sons of Shadows.

With every blow, they whittled the extremist group's strength, undoing its carefully laid plans, exposing

its twisted ideology. They faced the echoes of their

past head-on: they confronted the legacy of the Order of Shadows and it eventually got shattered.In the final

climactic confrontation, Mark, Lisa, and Rabbi Jacobson confronted Malakai, the deranged leader of the Sons of Shadows. Dark energy crackled around him as his eyes gleamed with an almost mad fervor.

But Mark, Lisa, and Rabbi Jacobson were older now, wiser and stronger in battle. They called upon some of the years that had bonded them through friendship and commitment to a common cause, an impenetrable shield against the darkness, firm in their resolve.

With those, he discharged a wave of combined energy-a surge of light cutting through the shadows, leaving Malakai defenseless. In one last scream of rage and frustration, the extremist leader's power finally crumbled under the weight of their collective strength.

The defeated and shattered remnants of the Sons of Shadows fled as the supernatural realm breathed a collective sigh of relief. The legacy of darkness had once again been confronted and defeated.

Mark, Lisa, Rabbi Jacobson, and Elena emerged from the catacombs, their spirits filled with both weariness and triumph. They had faced the echoes of the past, protected the fragile equilibrium they had fought so hard to establish, and paved the way for a future where light and darkness coexisted with balance.

In the aftermath of this battle, Mark, Lisa, and Rabbi Jacobson knew well that their time as guardians was coming to a close; they had played their mentor and protector roles well. The next generation was fully prepared to take up the baton of light. In Elena and many others inspired by them, their story would continue.

Mark, Lisa, and Rabbi Jacobson took the torch with a hopeful and grateful heart and passed it on to Elena,

asking her to take care of the world. She accepted

with modesty and determination to do the best she could in life, following the precepts of her teachers and

protecting the delicate balance between light and shadow.

And so, while the sun was setting over their guardian era, a new dawn began to rise. And the memories of Mark, Lisa, Rabbi Jacobson, and all who joined their cause

would always be within the pages of supernatural history. It was one of sacrifice, survival, and victory-what testimony to unity, love, and a resolute decision to keep at bay an encroaching shadow into the world.

Chapter 11: Resurfaced Shadows

In the aftermath of their victory against the Sons of Shadows, the supernatural realm found a semblance of peace once more. Mark, Lisa, and Rabbi Jacobson could rest easy, knowing the world they fought so desperately to save was at peace. But they understood that peace was often temporary, and the darkness found ways of surfacing at the most unwanted times.

A year had passed since the defeat of the extremist group, and the supernatural community had flourished. The alliances forged in the crucible of battle had grown stronger, beings from different realms working together to make sure that the balance between light and shadow remained intact.But then, whispers started to get around-

a growing unease that something was stirring in the dark. Strange occurrences, unexplained disappearances, and reports of dark energy emanating from the forgotten corners of the realm sent shivers down the spines of those who were attuned to such disturbances.

Mark, Lisa, and Rabbi Jacobson were ever watchful for the signs of an imminent danger. They once again rounded up their forces, prepared to meet whatever evil was lurking over the horizon. Elena, their protégée, had assumed her mantle as guardian, her powers whetted and her determination unshaken.

As the two stepped deep into the heart of the supernatural realm together, they chased threads of tenebrousness right from their sources. They would be guided into the very forgotten temple-long bathed in ancient power and cloaked from prying eyes where they were to face the resurfacing shades and finally the reason behind the new threat.

As they entered the temple, a chill settled in the air, the silence broken only by the soft echo of their footsteps. Symbols and sigils adorned the walls, pulsating with an eerie glow. The very essence of the temple seemed to breathe with anticipation, as if it had been waiting for their arrival.

Deep within the bowels of the temple, they found a

secret chamber. The air inside was thick with malevolent feelings, and a sense of doom hovered over

everything. Right in the middle of the chamber was a

strange altar with ancient runes around it and candles

of many colors flickering everywhere.

Mark, Lisa, and Rabbi Jacobson exchanged wary glances, their instincts telling them that disturbing the altar would have dire consequences. But they also knew that confronting the darkness required facing its source head-on. With a collective breath, they steeled themselves and approached the altar.

As they drew closer, a surge of dark energy crackled in the air, twisting and writhing around the altar. The shadows seemed to materialize, coalescing into a towering figure—a spectral being with eyes that burned with malice.

The being spoke in a voice that sent cold shivers down their spines, echoing within the chamber. "You have meddled in affairs beyond your comprehension," it hissed, its words dripping with contempt. "Prepare to face the consequences of your interference."

Mark, Lisa, Rabbi Jacobson, and Elena did not budge.

The attack was strong, but even then, the combined

energy, their shield, protected their ranks from the onslaught. Each strike that hit against the shield fueled their determination even more to overcome the malice in front of them.

United in a gesture of the most perfect unity, they fought back, focusing their combined powers on the entity. The chamber turned into a battlefield, with flashes of light and shadows interlacing in a crazy dance.

Every blow, every incantation, brought them closer to victory, even as the entity grew more desperate and vengeful.

But just when the battle was about to start going their way, the creature conjured a wave of darkness so powerful that it became apparent it would engulf them. Mark, Lisa, Rabbi Jacobson, and Elena stumbled, their defenses in ruins from the attack. They felt their strength fail and their spirits flickering as if from a dying flame.

It was then that an unlikely ally rose from the shadows, at least in my view, for this figure was full of secrets and power. Anaya-what a being. All this time, she silently watched the battle, seeking the right moment to disclose herself. With a commanding presence, she launched into the battle, merging her energy seamlessly with those of Mark, Lisa, Rabbi Jacobson, and Elena.

Anaya's arrival turned the tide of the battle. Her ancient knowledge and unparalleled abilities provided a renewed sense of hope. With her guidance, they reforged their defenses and launched a counterattack, their determination reignited.

The chamber shook, its very foundation trembling as it

fought to hold on to the world. But Mark, Lisa, Rabbi Jacobson, Elena, and Anaya all pressed onward, their collective unity creating a beacon in the light that pierced through an encroaching darkness.

In one last surge of energy, they struck the final blow, breaking through the entity's defenses and shattering its malevolent form. The chamber erupted in a blinding flash of light, dispelling the darkness that had sought to consume them.

As the light subsided, Mark, Lisa, Rabbi Jacobson, Elena, and Anaya stood victorious, their chests heaving with exertion and relief. The entity had been vanquished, its presence banished from the realm.

But the battle did leave its mark. The dark temple now pulsed with the essence of their victory; it stood as a living testament to their unyielding resolve and for their commitment to protect the world against the encroaching shadows.

At the exit from the temple, a renewed sense of purpose burned within them. The resurfacing shadows had been confronted and defeated, but they knew that darkness would always seek to reclaim its dominion. Their work was far from over, and they vowed to remain vigilant, ever ready to protect the delicate balance between light and shadow.

Mark, Lisa, Rabbi Jacobson, Elena, and Anaya

finally made it back to the supernatural community, and they were greeted with fanfare because this marked another victory over the resurfacing darkness. They shared their battle tale: the struggles and sacrifice it took to inspire others to stand against the shadows.

Along with the new comer to their ranks, a silent ally called Anaya, this made them almost unstoppable-hope to people who had gone off the rail, reminder to people that no matter the magnitude of darkness involved, unity coupled with unbreakable will always overcame it.

As the supernatural sphere basked in the afterglow of this victory, Mark, Lisa, Rabbi Jacobson, Elena, and Anaya were preparing themselves for what lay ahead. They knew the battle would never be fully won, for darkness would keep trying until it consumed the light-but with their shared strength, and the memories of battles won, they turned towards the future to protect their world from encroaching shadows once again.

Chapter 12: Shadows Unleashed

The war against darkness was over, but the supernatural world still hung in the balance. Mark, Lisa, Rabbi Jacobson, Elena, and Anaya knew the victory against the resurfacing shadows was just one step in a continuous struggle. They had seen the persistence of darkness, clawing its way back, seeking to regain its dominion.

News of their triumph spread like ripples in the supernatural community-minds both in awe and concern. The defeat of the resurfacing shadows had served to be a stark reminder of how fragile the balance between light and darkness was. Those who, over time, had become complacent with peace realized how close the threat lurking in the shadows actually was.

Mark, Lisa, Rabbi Jacobson, Elena, and Anaya knew well that their job was to confront not only the coming dangers but also to make sure the next generation was guided and prepared. They were bent upon seeing that the lessons learned from their battles would be passed to the next guardians for protecting the realm.

The resurfacing of the shadows led them to open an academy, a haven for learning and training. It was home to young supernaturals, coming to learn, in their training, and in deepening their understanding of the realm.

The academy became a place where different species and realms converged—a melting pot of cultures, traditions, and powers. Mark, Lisa, Rabbi Jacobson, Elena, and Anaya served as mentors and instructors, sharing their experiences and wisdom with the next generation.

Within the academy's walls, bonds were formed, friendships forged, and skills refined. Students from all walks of life learned from one another, embracing the diversity that made the supernatural realm so rich. They trained without rest, pushing their limits, and honing their abilities in preparation for the battles that lay ahead.

Over the years, the academy became a ray of hope, its reputation known far and wide. Supernaturals in all corners of the realm came to join its ranks, aspiring to be part of this community in protecting the world against the encroaching shadows.

Mark, Lisa, Rabbi Jacobson, Elena, and Anaya all made sure to extend the olive branch outside of the supernatural circles. They contacted human organizations that fought against supernatural threats and created alliances, sharing knowledge to help understand and cooperate with one another.

It wasn't long before their efforts did not go unnoticed. Governments, in their knowledge of the existence of the supernatural realm, sought their guidance in how to balance between the two worlds. Joint task forces were formed, comprising both supernaturals and humans working together in investigating and neutralizing supernatural threats. But not everyone

shared the love between humans and supernaturals. There were factions in both worlds that viewed the unity as a threat, believing the two realms should stay apart. Some humans were afraid of the unknown, while some

supernaturals harbored deep-seated resentment

toward humans.

Mark, Lisa, Rabbi Jacobson, Elena, and Anaya knew well how uphill their struggle was to get rid of these prejudices. They began a mission of goodwill and enlightenment, bridging the gulf between the two worlds. Their aim was to build an understanding, clear up some of the misconceptions, and establish a foundation for trust.

Because of this, they started to notice the perception change gradually. Humans and supernaturals found common ground: both wanted peace and security. Slowly, the barriers that had once divided them began to crumble, replaced by cooperation and mutual respect. Yet, even with their diplomatic efforts, another menace arose over the horizon: an ancient creature called the Shadow Sovereign. Legends spoke of an insatiable hunger for power, corrupting and manipulating the strongest beings.

Whispers of the awakening of the Shadow

Sovereign spread like a chilling wind throughout the supernatural world. Its malignant energy dripped into the hearts of the weak, stirring unrest and planting seeds of discontent. Mark, Lisa, Rabbi Jacobson, Elena, and Anaya knew the truth: it would take a coalition to defeat the Shadow Sovereign.

They marshaled their allies, drawing forces from various species, realms, and even human organizations. The academy became the nerve center of their operations as supernaturals and humans joined together, readying for the battle that would determine the fate of the realm.

It was time to face the Shadow Sovereign in a final confrontation that would try their combined strength and will. Mark, Lisa, Rabbi Jacobson, Elena, Anaya, and their allies traveled to a sacred site where the Shadow Sovereign had decided to manifest its full power.

Onward burst the Shadow Sovereign-the most huge figure, black with shadows that fairly bristled with bad intention, as the air weighed upon them. The air filled heavy with this oppression and supernaturally shook under the force.

Smoothing their resolution with determined eyes, Mark, Lisa, Rabbi Jacobson, Elena, and Anaya led the way forward by tapping their special powers. A very strong line of their people stood by their side and backed them against the advancement of these dark creatures. The battle that erupted was unlike any they had ever known. It was the first time the Shadow Sovereign used its power as a force of relentless fury against them, pouring waves of dark corruption into their ranks. Mark's fists shone with their ethereal light, hammering against the shadows. Lisa summoned the elements, control over fire, water, and earth, pushing back at the tendrils of the darkness. Rabbi Jacobson's prayers and sacred symbols formed a barrier of light, shielding their allies from the malevolent energy.

Elena, with her growing mastery of magic, cast spells that pierced the Shadow Sovereign's defenses, weakening its grip on the realm. Anaya's ancient knowledge and arcane abilities proved vital in unraveling the entity's complex weave of power, revealing its vulnerabilities.

The battle continued, both sides unleashing their fullest strengths. The clash of forces between the forces of light, which

provided hope, and the forces of consuming darkness

sent reverberations throughout the supernatural realm. They fought not only for their lives but for the very essence of their world.

With every strike, every incantation, the Shadow Sovereign's power waned. Mark, Lisa, Rabbi Jacobson, Elena, and Anaya pushed through exhaustion, their spirits fueled by the shared purpose of protecting the realm they held dear.

In one final, collective strike, they struck the blow that would exploit the weaknesses of the Shadow Sovereign. The entity recoiled, its dark form fracturing under the pressure. With a resounding cry, it dissipated, vanishing into the ether, its malevolent energy absorbed by the light that had united against it.

There was complete silence on the battlefield, save for the gentle whispers of the wind. The supernatural realm was at the threshold of its victory, the shadows quelled once more. Mark, Lisa, Rabbi Jacobson, Elena, Anaya, and their allies gathered their breath as their hearts swelled.

Chapter 13: Rebirth of Light

As the dust settled following their victory against the Shadow Sovereign, the supernatural realm was poised to enter a new era. Mark, Lisa, Rabbi Jacobson, Elena, Anaya, and their allies all exhaled a collective sigh of relief, their spirits buoyed by the triumph over darkness.

The battle had been fierce, stretching them to the breaking point of their strength and will. But they had emerged victorious, their unity and unwavering determination prevailing once more. They had proved very well that even in the face of overwhelming darkness, the light of hope could shine through.

Following the conflict, changes ran deep in the supernatural community. The defeat of the Shadow Sovereign was just a catalyst-the reminder of how fragile their realm was and how it needed cohesion in order to face adverse conditions.

Mark, Lisa, Rabbi Jacobson, Elena, and Anaya all

knew that their work was not done yet. They realized

that the task of healing and rebuilding needed to be

attended to, subsequent to the battle. All joined hands

for the purpose of restoring equilibrium and, by doing so, bringing a more robust supernatural realm into existence.

They turned to the communities that were suffering

under the influence of Shadow Sovereign, offering support and guidance. They listened to stories of those who had been touched by darkness, offering solace and reassurance. Through their compassion and understanding, they helped mend the wounds that the entity had inflicted.

The academy became a beacon of healing and learning, a haven for supernaturals seeking refuge and guidance. Mark, Lisa, Rabbi Jacobson, Elena, and Anaya poured their efforts into the academy, building up its curriculum and resources to better meet the needs of the supernatural community.

Jointly, they developed programs concentrated on self-discovery, emotional healing, and trauma recovery. They were cognizant that fighting against darkness leaves scars in hearts and minds, seen and unseen, of the people who stood and fought with them. The academy was a place of refuge where one would find the necessary support and tools to reclaim his sense of self and find strength in their vulnerabilities.

In their search to rebuild, Mark, Lisa, and Rabbi Jacobson looked toward the greater supernatural community. They worked tirelessly in bringing harmony, understanding, and cooperation between species and realms. By speaking openly and sharing experiences, they tried to dispel the mistrust and prejudices that had haunted their world for centuries.

Elena and Anaya, in their own unique ways, filled

very specific niches in these matters.

Elena, motivated by her experiences, became a spokesperson for the marginalized and an advocate for within the supernatural community. Anaya, meanwhile, tapped into her centuries-accumulated wisdom to be a liaison between worlds, sharing her insight and forging alliances.

The efforts of each were not without challenges. Lingering resentments and deeply ingrained prejudices

challenged their resolve. However, Mark, Lisa, Rabbi Jacobson, Elena, and Anaya remained steadfast, unwavering in their commitment to a brighter future.

As the supernatural community began to heal, their efforts garnered recognition beyond their own realm. Governments and organizations in the human world, witnessing the positive impact of their initiatives, sought their guidance in addressing supernatural-related issues. Collaborations between humans and supernaturals flourished, fostering greater understanding and cooperation.

Yet, in the midst of progress and healing, a new type of threat was whispered about. It reached the ears of Mark, Lisa, and Rabbi Jacobson that there was an ancient artifact capable of tilting the fragile balance between good and evil. They knew that their guardianship was never really done.

Guided by intuition and a feeling of urgency, they embarked on their quest to find and secure the artifact before it fell into bad hands. Elena and Anaya joined them, their experiences with each other forging an indelible bond. With them, they journeyed through dangerous land-scapes, unraveling ancient riddles and facing formidable challenges along the way.

Their journey took them to a secret haven, hidden from the world in a forgotten dimension. Here, in its halls of light, they finally found what they had been searching for: an artifact of awesome might-the "Tome of Shadows." Its dark energy pulsed ominously, a potentially catalyzing force for the return of darkness.

Realizing the danger of leaving such a powerful artifact unchecked, Mark, Lisa, Rabbi Jacobson, Elena, and Anaya devised a plan to contain its influence. They drew upon their collective knowledge and abilities, channeling the light within them to counteract the darkness of the Tome.

As they performed the intricate ritual, their combined energies formed a barrier, encasing the Tome and neutralizing its malevolent power. The artifact became inert, its potential for destruction contained.

But their success was short-lived. Behind their backs, there was a group of rogue supernaturals that had grown quite disillusioned with the new-found unity and the harmony they sought to foster; thus, they followed their every move. Their leader, the charismatic but deeply misguided Va-lerius, considered that the balance between light and darkness had gone so far into the light that the time was due to get back what he thought had been taken from him.

Valerius and his followers launched a surprise attack on

the sanctuary in pursuit of the Tome, intending to use its power to rewrite the supernatural realm according to their dark desires. A battle ensued, pitting the guardians of light against those who had succumbed to the seduction of darkness.

The bedlam everywhere and yet, in that, Mark stood with Lisa, Rabbi Jacobson, Elena, and Anaya, the chain unbroken. They fought back with a determined ferocity that had their need to keep the hard-won equilibrium.

As the battle raged on, Valerius, in his misplaced righteousness, engaged Mark in a final confrontation.

Chapter 14: The Crucible of Shadows

The clash of Mark and Valerius sent shock waves throughout the sanctuary, the impact of their powers making the very foundations shake. Their eyes met in a will-to-will combat, neither wanting to give in.

With an utterly misconceived belief, Valerius plunged into unleashing a tide of dark energy upon Mark. Tumbling and twisting around him were the shades in grotesque capering. Yet Mark did not bend, the light at his center keeping him stalwart, like a point of resistance to the insidious invading dark.

Their powers met, and the air crackled with an almost palpable tension as forces of light and darkness foughtfor dominance. The consequence of their battle would be the determination of the fate of not only the sanctuary but also the delicate balance in the supernatural realm.

Meanwhile, Lisa, Rabbi Jacobson, Elena, and Anaya fought valiantly against the followers of Valerius.

Noises of the fight resounded in the hall: spells and incantations intertwined with the clashing of weapons.

Every member of the group used their unique abilities, smoothly combining their attacks and covering each other's backs.

Elena, in particular, turned out to be a very powerful witch, who channeled her energy to create protective shields and launch potent magical assaults against their adversaries. Anaya used her ancient wisdom to employ

arcane knowledge in unraveling the dark spells woven by Valerius's followers, leaving them vulnerable to the group's onslaught.

Meanwhile, the battle raged, as blurred lines between light and darkness seemed to struggle within the sanctuary; it was a test of strength, courage, and will, each fighting for their kind of future.

As Mark and Valerius clashed, the room around them shook with the strain of their powers. Mark, drawing from the battles he had been through, took the energy of his allies and combined their strengths with his. The light within him grew in intensity, trying to force its way against the darkness that was Valerius.

Valerius, aware of his defeat, became all the more desperate; his attacks began to be wild. In his last, desperate, big surge of power, he struck out to destroy Mark and the sanctuary for his own purposes.

But when the odds were really against him, Mark found a

different determination. He drew from deep within himself, his spirit mingling with the light around him. With a sudden burst of will, he turned Valerius's attack, using its momentum against him.

The tables had turned, and it was Valerius' time to be at the mercy of Mark's power. The darkness which had consumed him thus began to wane, weakened by the light that now enveloped him. In that instant, Mark reached out an open hand to give Valerius another chance.

And when pride had been shattered and beliefs

shaken, Valerius hesitated. For a minute, the battle had graphically shown him the result of what he had done: his misguided pursuit of power I

nto chaos within the supernatural realm. Slowly, he extended his hand and grasped Mark's, opting for the path of redemption against the path of destruction.

As their hands connected, a surge of energy pulsed through them both. The darkness within Valerius dissolved, replaced by a flickering light. It was a moment of transformation, as Valerius embraced the possibility of change, recognizing the error of his ways.

With Valerius' defeat, the other forces of darkness began to falter. Lisa, Rabbi Jacobson, Elena, and Anaya continued to press their advantage until it became overwhelming for their adversaries. The sanctuary echoed with the sounds of defeat as the remaining followers of Valerius fled or surrendered, their hopes of supremacy dashed.

The room fell into a tense silence, broken only by the labored breaths of the weary combatants. Mark and Valerius stood before each other, their eyes reflecting a mixture of weariness and newfound understanding. Valerius spoke in a soft voice, laced with remorse. "I see now the folly of my ways. The pursuit of power led me astray, but you have shown me the path to redemption. I vow to dedicate my life to restoring the balance, to righting the wrongs I have committed."

Mark nodded, taking Valerius's pledge. "Salvation is at hand for those who wish it. But let it be known that the road ahead shall not be easy.

One must be avowed to the light, in eternal combat against the darkness within. Will you accept that? "

Valerius nodded, his eyes now shining with a fresh resolve. "I am ready to face the crucible of shadows and emerge on the side of light."

As it is said, my enemies are now allies. Mark, Lisa, Rabbi Jacobson, Elena, Anaya, and Valerius turn to deal with the post-battle situation. The sanctuary bears heavy bruises from the war, so all of them teamed up their efforts to fix broken walls and clean off remnants of darkness.

As they worked together, they talked about forgiveness and a possible redemption within the supernatural realm; that everyone-despite who had fallen into darkness-deserved a chance to find their way back into the light. It was a testament to the power of unity, compassion, and the capacity for change.

As a result of the victory, the supernatural world went through a great change. Mark, Lisa, Rabbi Jacobson, Elena, Anaya, and Valerius' union became a beacon of hope, redemption, and the will to change and build a new future.

Together, they vowed to work at rebuilding the balance, making stronger the bonds between supernatural beings and creating awareness between their world and humans. They worked together to see that the lessons from their battles were not forgotten and that their legacy of unity and resilience endured.

Now that Valerius stood with them, the group sealed a pact-a promise of cooperation to help keep the universal balance between light and darkness intact. They realized that their journey was not yet complete and that their victories against the Shadow Sovereign and the followers of Valerius were only steps in a greater battle.

As they reassembled, Mark, Lisa, Rabbi Jacobson, Elena, Anaya, and Valerius discussed their next course of action. They realized that the supernatural realm was still fraught with threats within and outside its borders and that they would have to be vigilant to face any challenge that might arise.

Humbled by the knowledge of his past transgressions, Valerius became a spokesman for change among supernatural society. Using his experiences as a cautionary tale, Valerius told and retold the story of his redemption and of the dangers of falling prey to darkness. And in it, those supernatural beings that had ever flirted with the edges of despair found their hope,

their route back towards redemption.

Together, they devised a plan to establish a council-a unified governing body that would bring together representatives from various supernatural species and realms. It would serve as an open forum for discussion and decision-making, a method of conflict resolution. In this way, it would provide a forum for collaboration and unity on all levels, so that the needs and concerns of all would be heard and addressed.

Mark, Lisa, Rabbi Jacobson, Elena, Anaya, and Valerius became the founding members of this council, with the combination of their wisdom and experiences guiding its formation. They then extended an invitation to all other leaders of the different supernatural factions to join the council and work for the betterment of their realm.

With this establishment of the council, the world witnessed a new beginning for Supernatural Life.

In that council, what created the environment of co-operation-which meant negotiating problems out, not violence-supernaturals that had stood so long against one another for and by themselves, started finding

common grounds on to what a perfect world would be like.

The council also worked to further the connection between the supernatural and human worlds. Mark, Lisa, and

Rabbi Jacobson had learned from experience thatthere was much to be gained from insight and cooperation between the two worlds. They held forums and conferences, gathering representatives from both sides to discuss common problems and possible avenues of collaboration.

It was through such efforts that bridges were formed, and trust started to develop between them. Humans came to admire the depth of cultures and powers within the realm of the supernatural, just as supernaturals learned to appreciate the ingenuity

and resolute spirit of humans. Eventually, barriers faded between both worlds, allowing a new form of coexistence to dawn.

As the council, along with its initiatives, gained momentum, Mark, Lisa, and Rabbi Jacobson realized that indeed their role as guardians itself was evolving. They had planted the seeds of change, and now it was time to nurture their growth. They shifted their attention to mentorship-guiding the next generation of protectors-and prepared them for the challenges that lay ahead.

What was once a sanctuary that had nurtured healing now acted as a training field for guardians-in-training. Mark, Lisa, Rabbi Jacobson, Elena, Anaya, and Valerius became teachers of many, sharing their knowledge,

further developing the skills of the young supernaturals, teaching them what they had learned in battle.

The academy was alive with young supernaturals from all walks of life training side by side, extending their limits, perfecting their abilities, and wearing the responsibility that came with their powers. Bonds were formed, friendships grew, and in-walls camaraderie blossomed.

Meanwhile, Mark, Lisa, and Rabbi Jacobson continued to refine their own abilities, delving deeper into the mysteries of the supernatural realm. They sought out ancient texts, consulted wise elders, and journeyed to sacred sites, all in an effort to expand their understanding and unlock new layers of power.

In their search for knowledge, they found a prophecy-a message vague yet hinting at an imminent peril. It spoke of forces converging, a storm gathering that would test the very substance of the supernatural world. They realized that their battles against the Shadow Sovereign and Valerius's followers were merely preludes to a greater conflict.

With this knowledge, Mark, Lisa, Rabbi Jacobson, Elena, Anaya, and Valerius rallied the council and the supernatural community to prepare for the impending storm. They held training sessions, devised contingency plans, and strengthened their alliances in preparation.

The supernatural realm braced itself, united as one against an uncertain future. Mark, Lisa, Rabbi Jacobson, Elena, Anaya, and Valerius were in the lead, their firm determination inspiring others to rise to the challenge.

And so, while the realm prepared for the storm, a sense of purpose and hope would pervade the air; the battles they had fought, the alliances they had forged, and the lessons they had learned turned them into guardians of light. They were ready to face whatever darkness awaited them, knowing that together they were stronger and that their commitment to unity and resilience would guide them through the crucible of shadows.

Chapter 15: The Final Confrontation

The supernatural realm braced itself as the prophesied storm loomed on the horizon. Mark, Lisa, Rabbi Jacobson, Elena, Anaya, Valerius, and the council had rallied the supernatural community, preparing them for the final battle against an ancient and malevolent force.

Whispers of this impending threat echoed through the realm, spreading a sense of unease and anticipation. Supernaturals from all walks of life trained rigorously, honing their skills and fortifying their defenses. The academy buzzed with activity as the next generation of guardians prepared to stand alongside their mentors in the face of darkness.

Within the council chambers, Mark, Lisa, Rabbi Jacobson, Elena, Anaya, and Valerius convened. They pored over ancient texts, deciphering cryptic prophecies and seeking insights into the nature of the approaching threat. Their discussions were filled with urgency, each member sharing their knowledge and devising strategies to counteract the impending darkness.

Their research led them to a forgotten temple, hidden deep within a forbidden realm. Legends spoke of a dark entity, known as the Ebonheart, whose power rivaled that of the Shadow Sovereign. They believed that this ancient force had awoken, seeking to plunge the supernatural realm into eternal darkness.

With a sense of purpose, the group embarked on a treacherous journey to confront the Ebonheart. They traversed treacherous terrains, braving harsh climates and facing formidable obstacles. Their bond and shared determination carried them forward, overcoming every challenge that stood in their path.

As they arrived at the temple, a foreboding aura enveloped them. The air crackled with an electric charge, and an eerie silence settled upon the group. They approached the temple entrance cautiously, fully aware of the darkness that awaited them within.

The temple's interior was bathed in shadow, its architecture an intricate tapestry of malevolence. Candles flickered, casting dancing shadows on the walls as the group delved deeper into the heart of darkness. Their footsteps echoed ominously, each step a testament to their courage and resolve.

Within the inner sanctum, they encountered the Ebonheart—a looming figure cloaked in darkness. Its presence was suffocating, its eyes burning with an otherworldly intensity. A voice, dripping with venom, echoed through the chamber, reverberating in their souls.

"Fools! You dare challenge the might of the Ebonheart? Your futile resistance shall only hasten your demise," the entity hissed, its voice resonating with a sinister authority.

Mark stepped forward, his voice steady and filled with unwavering conviction. "We stand united, guided by the light that resides within us. Your reign of darkness ends here, Ebonheart. We will not falter in the face of your malevolence."

With those words, the battle erupted in a whirlwind of light and darkness. The clash of powers sent shock waves through the temple, each strike threatening to consume the other. Mark, Lisa, Rabbi Jacobson, Elena, Anaya, and Valerius fought valiantly, utilizing their individual strengths while maintaining the unity that had brought them this far.

Mark's fists blazed with ethereal light, striking at the heart of the Ebonheart's shadows. Lisa's mastery over the elements conjured gusts of wind and torrents of flame, pushing back against the entity's oppressive darkness. Rabbi Jacobson's prayers resonated with divine energy, forming a barrier of light that shielded their allies from the Ebonheart's attacks.

Elena, drawing upon her growing magical prowess, cast spells that unraveled the Ebonheart's defenses, weakening its hold on the realm. Anaya, with her ancient wisdom and arcane abilities, provided crucial guidance, exploiting the entity's vulnerabilities and revealing its hidden weaknesses.

As the battle raged on, the Ebonheart grew more desperate, its attacks becoming increasingly fierce and unpredictable. It summoned shadowy minions, each one embodying a fragment of its immense power. The group found themselves overwhelmed, outnumbered by the relentless onslaught.

But they refused to yield. Mark, Lisa, Rabbi Jacobson, Elena, Anaya, and Valerius drew strength from one another, their bonds fortified in the crucible of battle. With unwavering determination, they launched a coordinated assault, targeting the Ebonheart's core.

As they fought, their powers intertwined, creating a symphony of light that pierced through the entity's darkness. The Ebonheart, weakened by their relentless assault, faltered, its form trembling with the strain.

In a final surge of energy, the group unleashed their combined might, channeling their collective power into a single, concentrated strike. Light erupted in an explosion of brilliance, engulfing the Ebonheart and shattering its malevolent form.

The temple quaked as the darkness dissipated, leaving behind only echoes of the entity's former presence. The supernatural realm breathed a collective sigh of relief, the weight of darkness finally lifted. The Ebonheart had been vanquished, its power reduced to mere echoes of a forgotten time.

Exhausted but triumphant, Mark, Lisa, Rabbi Jacobson, Elena, Anaya, and Valerius emerged from the temple, their steps heavy but filled with newfound hope. They had overcome the greatest threat the supernatural realm had faced, proving that unity and resilience could triumph over even the darkest of forces.

The supernatural community celebrated their victory, acknowledging the sacrifices made and the indomitable spirit that had led them to this moment. Mark, Lisa, Rabbi Jacobson, Elena, Anaya, and Valerius were hailed as heroes, their names etched into the annals of supernatural history.

But they knew their work was not yet done. The battles they had fought had forged them into a formidable force, one capable of defending the realm from any future threats. They vowed to remain ever vigilant, their commitment to protecting the balance between light and darkness unwavering.

Chapter 12: Shadows Unleashed

The war against darkness was over, but the supernatural world still hung in the balance. Mark, Lisa, Rabbi Jacobson, Elena, and Anaya knew the victory against the resurfacing shadows was just one step in a continuous struggle. They had seen the persistence of darkness, clawing its way back, seeking to regain its dominion.

News of their triumph spread like ripples in the supernatural community-minds both in awe and concern. The defeat of the resurfacing shadows had served to be a stark reminder of how fragile the balance between light and darkness was. Those who, over time, had become complacent with peace realized how close the threat lurking in the shadows actually was.

Mark, Lisa, Rabbi Jacobson, Elena, and Anaya knew well that their job was to confront not only the coming dangers but also to make sure the next generation was guided and prepared. They were bent upon seeing that the lessons learned from their battles would be passed to the next guardians

for protecting the realm.

The resurfacing of the shadows led them to open an academy, a haven for learning and training. It was home to young supernaturals, coming to learn, in their training, and in deepening their understanding of the realm.

The academy became a place where different species and realms converged—a melting pot of cultures, traditions, and powers. Mark, Lisa, Rabbi Jacobson, Elena, and Anaya served as mentors and instructors, sharing their experiences and wisdom with the next generation.

Within the academy's walls, bonds were formed, friendships forged, and skills refined. Students from all walks of life learned from one another, embracing the diversity that made the supernatural realm so rich. They trained without rest, pushing their limits, and honing their abilities in preparation for the battles that lay ahead.

Over the years, the academy became a ray of hope, its reputation known far and wide. Supernaturals in all corners of the realm came to join its ranks, aspiring to be part of this community in protecting the world against the encroaching shadows.

Mark, Lisa, Rabbi Jacobson, Elena, and Anaya all made sure to extend the olive branch

outside of the supernatural circles. They contacted human organizations that fought against supernatural threats and created alliances, sharing knowledge to help understand and cooperate with one another.

It wasn't long before their efforts did not go unnoticed. Governments, in their knowledge of the existence of the supernatural realm, sought their guidance in how to balance between the two worlds. Joint task forces were formed, comprising both supernaturals and humans working together in investigating and neutralizing supernatural threats.

But not everyone shared the love between humans and supernaturals. There were factions in both worlds that viewed the unity as a threat, believing the two realms should stay apart. Some humans were afraid of the unknown, while some supernaturals harbored deep-seated resentment toward humans.

Mark, Lisa, Rabbi Jacobson, Elena, and Anaya knew well how uphill their struggle was to get rid of these prejudices. They began a mission of goodwill and enlightenment, bridging the gulf between the two worlds. Their aim was to build an understanding, clear up some of the misconceptions, and establish a foundation for trust.

Because of this, they started to notice the perception

change gradually. Humans and supernaturals found common ground: both wanted peace and security. Slowly, the barriers that had once divided them began to crumble, replaced by cooperation and mutual respect.

Yet, even with their diplomatic efforts, another menace arose over the horizon: an ancient creature called the Shadow Sovereign.

Legends spoke of an insatiable hunger for power, corrupting and manipulating the strongest beings.

Whispers of the awakening of the Shadow

Sovereign spread like a chilling wind throughout the supernatural world. Its malignant energy dripped into the hearts of the weak, stirring unrest and planting seeds of discontent. Mark, Lisa, Rabbi Jacobson, Elena, and Anaya knew the truth: it would take a coalition to defeat the Shadow Sovereign.

They marshaled their allies, drawing forces from various species, realms, and even human organizations. The academy became the nerve center of their operations as supernaturals and humans joined together, readying for the battle that would determine the fate of the realm.

It was time to face the Shadow Sovereign in a final confrontation that would try their combined strength and will. Mark, Lisa, Rabbi Jacobson, Elena, Anaya, and their allies traveled to a sacred site where the

Shadow Sovereign had decided to manifest its full power.

Onward burst the Shadow Sovereign-the most huge figure, black with shadows that fairly bristled with bad intention, as the air weighed upon them. The air filled heavy with this oppression and supernaturally shook under the force.

Smoothing their resolution with determined eyes, Mark, Lisa, Rabbi Jacobson, Elena, and Anaya led the way forward by tapping their special powers. A very strong line of their people stood by their side and backed them against the advancement of these dark creatures.

The battle that erupted was unlike any they had ever known. It was the first time the Shadow Sovereign used its power as a force of relentless fury against them, pouring waves of dark corruption into their ranks. Mark's fists shone with their ethereal light, hammering against the shadows. Lisa summoned the elements, control over fire, water, and earth, pushing back at the tendrils of the darkness. Rabbi Jacobson's prayers and sacred symbols formed a barrier of light, shielding their allies from the malevolent energy.

Elena, with her growing mastery of magic, cast spells that pierced the Shadow Sovereign's defenses, weakening its grip on the realm. Anaya's ancient knowledge and arcane abilities proved vital in unraveling the entity's complex weave of power, revealing its vulnerabilities.

The battle continued, both sides unleashing their fullest strengths. The clash of forces between the forces of light, which provided hope, and the forces of consuming darkness sent reverberations throughout the supernatural realm. They fought not only for their lives but for the very essence of their world. With every strike, every incantation, the Shadow Sovereign's power waned. Mark, Lisa, Rabbi Jacobson, Elena, and Anaya pushed through exhaustion, their spirits fueled by the shared purpose of protecting the realm they held dear.

In one final, collective strike, they struck the blow that would exploit the weaknesses of the Shadow Sovereign. The entity recoiled, its dark form fracturing under the pressure. With a resounding cry, it dissipated, vanishing into the ether, its malevolent energy absorbed by the light that had united against it.

There was complete silence on the battlefield, save for the gentle whispers of the wind. The supernatural realm was at the threshold of its victory, the shadows quelled once more. Mark, Lisa, Rabbi Jacobson, Elena, Anaya, and their allies gathered their breath as their hearts swelled.

Chapter 13: Rebirth of Light

As the dust settled following their victory against the Shadow Sovereign, the supernatural realm was poised to enter a new era. Mark, Lisa, Rabbi Jacobson, Elena, Anaya, and their allies all exhaled a collective sigh of relief, their spirits buoyed by the triumph over darkness.

The battle had been fierce, stretching them to the breaking point of their strength and will. But they had emerged victorious, their unity and unwavering determination prevailing once more. They had proved very well that even in the face of overwhelming darkness, the light of hope could shine through.

Following the conflict, changes ran deep in the

supernatural community. The defeat of the Shadow Sovereign was just a catalyst-the reminder of how fragile their realm was and how it needed cohesion in order to face adverse conditions.

Mark, Lisa, Rabbi Jacobson, Elena, an Anaya all knew that their work was not done yet. They realized that the task of healing and rebuilding needed to be attended to, subsequent to the battle. All joined hands or the

purpose of restoring equilibrium and, by doing so, bringing a more robust supernatural realm into existence.

They turned to the communities that were suffering under

the influence of Shadow Sovereign, offering support and guidance. They listened to stories of those who had been touched by darkness, offering solace and reassurance. Through their compassion and understanding, they helped mend the wounds that the entity had inflicted.

The academy became a beacon of healing and learning, a haven for supernaturals seeking refuge and guidance. Mark, Lisa, Rabbi Jacobson, Elena, and Anaya poured their efforts into the academy, building up its curriculum and resources to better meet the needs of the supernatural community.

Jointly, they developed programs concentrated on self-discovery, emotional healing, and trauma recovery. They were cognizant that fighting against darkness leaves scars in hearts and minds, seen and unseen, of the people who stood and fought with them.

The academy was a place of refuge where one would find the necessary support and tools to reclaim his sense of

self and find strength in their vulnerabilities.

In their search to rebuild, Mark, Lisa, and Rabbi Jacobson looked toward the greater supernatural community. They worked tirelessly in bringing harmony, understanding, and cooperation between species and realms. By speaking openly and sharing experiences, they tried to dispel the mistrust and prejudices that had haunted their world for centuries.

Elena and Anaya, in their own unique ways, filled very specific niches in these matters. Elena, motivated by her experiences, became a spokesperson for the marginalized and an advocate for inclusivity within the supernatural community. Anaya, meanwhile, tapped into her centuries-accumulated wisdom to be a liaison between worlds, sharing her insight and forging alliances.

The efforts of each were not without challenges. Lingering resentments and deeply engrained prejudices challenged their resolve. However, Mark, Lisa, Rabbi Jacobson, Elena, and Anaya remained steadfast, unwavering in their commitment to a brighter future.

As the supernatural community began to heal, their efforts garnered recognition beyond their own realm. Governments and organizations in the human world, witnessing the positive impact of their initiatives, sought their guidance in addressing supernatural-related issues. Collaborations between humans and supernaturals flourished, fostering greater understanding and cooperation.

Yet, in the midst of progress and healing, a new type of threat was whispered about. It reached the ears of Mark, Lisa, and Rabbi Jacobson that there was an

ancient artifact capable of tilting the fragile balance between good and evil. They knew that their guardianship was never really done.

Guided by intuition and a feeling of urgency, they embarked on their quest to find and secure the artifact before it fell into bad hands. Elena and Anaya joined them, their experiences with each other forgingan indelible bond. With them, they journeyed through dangerous landscapes, unraveling ancient riddles and facing formidable challenges along the way.

Their journey took them to a secret haven, hidden from the world in a forgotten dimension. Here, in its halls of light, they finally found what they had been searching for: an artifact of awesome might-the "Tome of Shadows." Its dark energy pulsed ominously, a potentially catalyzing force for the return of darkness.

Realizing the danger of leaving such a powerful artifact unchecked, Mark, Lisa, Rabbi Jacobson, Elena, and

Anaya devised a plan to contain its influence. They drew upon their collective knowledge and abilities, channeling the light within them to counteract the darkness of the Tome.

As they performed the intricate ritual, their combined energies formed a barrier, encasing the Tome and neutralizing its malevolent power. The artifact became inert, its potential for destruction contained.

But their success was short-lived. Behind their backs,

there was a group of rogue supernaturals that had grown quite disillusioned with the newfound unity and the harmony they sought to foster; thus, they followed their every move. Their leader, the charismatic but deeply misguided Valerius, considered that the balance between light and darkness had gone so far into the light that the time was due to get back what he thought had been taken from him.

Valerius and his followers launched a surprise attack on the sanctuary in pursuit of the Tome, intending to use its power to rewrite the supernatural realm according to their dark desires. A battle ensued, pitting the guardians of light against those who had succumbed to the seduction of darkness.

The bedlam everywhere and yet, in that, Mark stood with Lisa, Rabbi Jacobson, Elena, and Anaya, the chain

unbroken. They fought back with a determined ferocity that had their need to keep the hard-won equilibrium.

As the battle raged on, Valerius, in his misplaced righteousness, engaged Mark in a final confrontation. The powers cla

Chapter 14

The clash of Mark and Valerius sent shock waves throughout the sanctuary, the impact of their powers making the very foundations shake. Their eyes met in a will-to-will combat, neither wanting to give in.

With an utterly misconceived belief, Valerius plunged into unleashing a tide of dark energy upon Mark. Tumbling and twisting around him were the shades in grotesque capering. Yet Mark did not bend, the light at his center keeping him stalwart, like a point of resistance to the insidious invading dark.

Their powers met, and the air crackled with an almost palpable tension as forces of light and darkness fought for dominance. The consequence of their battle would be the determination of the fate of not only the sanctuary but also the delicate balance in the supernatural realm.

Meanwhile, Lisa, Rabbi Jacobson, Elena, and Anaya fought valiantly against the followers of Valerius. Noises of the fight resounded in the hall: spells and incantations intertwined with the clashing of weapons. Every member of the group used their unique abilities, smoothly combining their attacks and covering each other's backs.

Elena, in particular, turned out to be a very powerful witch, who channeled her energy to create protective shields and launch potent magical assaults against their adversaries. Anaya used her ancient wisdom to employ.

arcane knowledge in unraveling the dark spells woven by Valerius's followers, leaving them vulnerable to the group's onslaught.

Meanwhile, the battle raged, as blurred lines between light and darkness seemed to struggle within the sanctuary; it was a test of strength, courage, and will, each fighting for their kind of future.

As Mark and Valerius clashed, the room around them shook with the strain of their powers. Mark, drawing from the battles he had been through, took the energy of his allies and combined their strengths with his. The light within him grew in intensity, trying to force its way against the darkness that was Valerius.

Valerius, aware of his defeat, became all the more desperate; his attacks began to be wild. In his last, desperate, big surge of power, he struck out to destroy Mark and the sanctuary for his own purposes.

But when the odds were really against him, Mark found a different determination. He drew from deep within himself, his spirit mingling with the light around him. With a sudden burst of will, he turned Valerius's attack, using its momentum against him.

The tables had turned, and it was Valerius' time to be at the mercy of Mark's power. The darkness which had consumed him thus began to wane, weakened by the light that now enveloped him. In that instant, Mark reached out an open hand to give Valerius another chance.

And when pride had been shattered and beliefs shaken,Valerius hesitated. For a minute, the battle had graphically shown him the result of what he had done: his misguided pursuit of power into chaos within the supernatural realm. Slowly, he extended his hand and grasped Mark's, opting for the path of redemption against the path of destruction.

As their hands connected, a surge of energy pulsed through them both. The darkness within Valerius dissolved, replaced by a flickering light. It was a moment of transformation, as Valerius embraced the possibility of change, recognizing the error of his ways.

With Valerius' defeat, the other forces of darkness began to falter. Lisa,

Rabbi Jacobson, Elena, and Anaya continued to press their advantage until it became overwhelming for their adversaries. The sanctuary echoed with the sounds of defeat as the remaining followers of Valerius fled or surrendered, their hopes of supremacy dashed.

The room fell into a tense silence, broken only by the labored breaths of the weary combatants. Mark and Valerius stood before each other, their eyes reflecting a mixture of weariness and newfound understanding.

Valerius spoke in a soft voice, laced with remorse. "I see now the folly of my ways. The pursuit of power led me astray, but you have shown me the path to redemption. I vow to dedicate my life to restoring the balance, to righting the wrongs I have committed."

Mark nodded, taking Valerius's pledge. "Salvation is at hand for those who wish it. But let it be known that the road ahead shall not be easy. One must be avowed to the light, in eternal combat against the darkness within.

Will you accept that? "

Valerius nodded, his eyes now shining with a fresh resolve. "I am ready to face the crucible of shadows and emerge on the side of light."

As it is said, my enemies are now allies. Mark, Lisa, Rabbi Jacobson, Elena, Anaya, and Valerius turn to deal with the post-battle situation. The sanctuary bears heavy bruises from the war, so all of them teamed up their efforts to fix broken walls and clean off remnants of darkness.

As they worked together, they talked about forgiveness and a possible redemption within the supernatural realm; that everyone-despite who had fallen into darkness-deserved a chance to find their way back into the light. It was a testament to the power of unity, compassion, and the capacity for change.

As a result of the victory, the supernatural world went

through a great change. Mark, Lisa, Rabbi Jacobson, Elena, Anaya, and Valerius' union became a beacon of hope, redemption, and the will to change and build a new future.

Together, they vowed to work at rebuilding the balance, making stronger the bonds between supernatural beings and creating awareness between their world and humans. They worked together to see that the lessons from their battles were not forgotten and that their legacy of unity and resilience endured.

Now that Valerius stood with them, the group sealed a pact-a promise of cooperation to help keep the universal balance between light and darkness intact. They realized that their journey was not yet complete and that their victories against the Shadow Sovereign and the followers of Valerius were only steps in a greater battle.

As they reassembled, Mark, Lisa, Rabbi Jacobson, Elena, Anaya, and Valerius discussed their next course of action. They realized that the supernatural realm was still fraught with threats within and outside its borders and that they would have to be vigilantto face any challenge that might arise.

Humbled by the knowledge of his past transgressions, Valerius became a spokesman for change among supernatural society. Using his experiences as a cautionary tale, Valerius told and retold the story of his redemption and of the dangers of falling prey to darkness. And in it, those supernatural beings that had ever flirted with the edges of despair found their hope, their route back towards redemption.

Together, they devised a plan to establish a council-a unified governing body that would bring together representatives from various supernatural species and realms. It would serve as an open forum for discussion and decision-making, a method of conflict resolution. In this way, it would provide a forum for collaboration and unity on all levels, so that the needs and concerns of all would be heard and addressed.

Mark, Lisa, Rabbi Jacobson, Elena, Anaya, and Valerius became the founding members of this council, with the combination of their wisdom and experiences guiding its formation. They then extended an invitation to all other leaders of the different supernatural factions to join the council and work for the betterment of their realm.

With this establishment of the council, the world witnessed
a new beginning for Supernatural Life.

In that council, what created the environment of co-operation-which meant negotiating problems out, not

violence-supernaturals that had stood so long against one another for and by themselves, started finding

common grounds on to what a perfect world would be like.

The council also worked to further the connection between the supernatural and human worlds. Mark, Lisa, and Rabbi Jacobson had learned from experience that there was much to be gained from insight and co-operation between the two worlds. They held forums and conferences, gathering representatives from both sides to discuss common problems and possible avenues of collaboration.

It was through such efforts that bridges were formed, and trust started to develop between them. Humans came to admire the depth of cultures and powers within the realm of the supernatural, just as supernaturals learned to appreciate the ingenuity and resolute spirit of humans. Eventually, barriers faded between both worlds, allowing a new form of coexistence to dawn.

As the council, along with its initiatives, gained momentum, Mark, Lisa, and Rabbi Jacobson realized that indeed their role as guardians itself was evolving. They had planted the seeds of change, and now it was time to nurture their growth. They shifted their attention to mentorship-guiding the next generation of protectors-and prepared them for the challenges that lay ahead.

What was once a sanctuary that had nurtured healing now acted as a training field for guardians-in-training. Mark, Lisa, Rabbi Jacobson, Elena, Anaya, and Valerius became teachers of many, sharing their knowledge, further developing the skills of the young supernaturals, teaching them what they had learned in battle.

The academy was alive with young supernaturals from all walks of life training side by side, extending their limits, perfecting their abilities, and wearing the responsibility that came with their powers. Bonds were formed, friendships grew, and in-walls camaraderie blossomed.

Meanwhile, Mark, Lisa, and Rabbi Jacobson continued to refine their own abilities, delving deeper into the mysteries of the supernatural realm. They sought out ancient texts, consulted wise elders, and journeyed to sacred sites, all in an effort to expand their understanding and unlock new layers of power.

In their search for knowledge, they found a prophecy-a message vague yet hinting at an imminent peril. It spoke of forces converging, a storm gathering that would test the very substance of the supernatural world. They realized that their battles against the Shadow Sovereign and Valerius's followers were merely preludes to a greater conflict.

With this knowledge, Mark, Lisa, Rabbi Jacobson, Elena, Anaya, and Valerius rallied the council and the supernatural community to prepare for the impending storm. They held training sessions, devised contingency plans, and strengthened their alliances in preparation.

The supernatural realm braced itself, united as one against an uncertain future. Mark, Lisa, Rabbi Jacobson, Elena, Anaya, and Valerius were in the lead, their firm determination inspiring others to rise to the challenge.

And so, while the realm prepared for the storm, a sense of purpose and hope would pervade the air; the battles they had fought, the alliances they had forged, and the lessons they had learned turned them into guardians of light. They were ready to face whatever darkness awaited them, knowing that together they were stronger and that their commitment to unity and resilience would guide them through the crucible of shadows.

www.ingramcontent.com/pod-product-compliance
Lightning Source LLC
Chambersburg PA
CBHW061256140726
47998CB00006B/2235